FALL OF THE REAPER

Witch of the Lake Book Three

MIRANDA HONFLEUR
NICOLETTE ANDREWS

"A mythic delight and new release you must read... For those who love stories with well-woven mythologies, this is a wonderful tale. It draws from Polish mythology, and features a well-crafted Eastern European world, complete with a foreboding forest, Mrok witches, and strange denizens of the deep which demand justice for murdered women."

— J.M. BUTLER, AUTHOR OF THE TUE-RAH CHRONICLES

"*Feast of the Mother* is a delightfully magical old-world fantasy. With a heroine who is both grave and valiant, a world full of mystery and haunting magic, and a mystery that will keep you riveted, you won't be able to put down this delightful tale. Recommended for fans of *An Enchantment of Ravens*. Don't miss this triumphant first-in-series by authors Miranda Honfleur and Nicolette Andrews."

— SARAH K. L. WILSON, BESTSELLING AUTHOR OF THE DRAGON SCHOOL SERIES

"Completely unlike anything I expected or anything I've read before. Brygida is a witch who is only beginning to know what she's capable of and what her duties are. She's a fantastic character, strong in her convictions and loyal in her beliefs. I can't help but root for someone like that. And this world! It's so intriguing and fun that I flew through the pages, not wanting to stop. Utterly fascinating! With a slow burn romance, well-developed world, and beautiful prose, this is a story that should not be missed."

— M. LYNN, BESTSELLING AUTHOR
OF THE FANTASY AND FAIRYTALES
SERIES

Cover art by KD Ritchie at Storywrappers

Map by Rela "Kellerica" Similä

Proofreading by Anthony S. Holabird

Paperback ISBN: 978-1-949932-22-5

ALSO BY MIRANDA HONFLEUR

Blade and Rose Series

"Winter Wren" (available on www.mirandahonfleur.com)

Blade & Rose (Book 1)

By Dark Deeds (Book 2)

Court of Shadows (Book 3)

Blade and Rose: Books 1-3 Digital Boxed Set

Queen of the Shining Sea (Book 4)

The Dragon King (Book 5) Available 2020*

Immortelle (Book 6) Available 2020*

The Dark-Elves of Nightbloom Series

No Man Can Tame (Book 1)

Bright of the Moon (Book 2) forthcoming*

Crown To Ashes (Book 3) forthcoming*

The Curse of the Fae Lord Series

Dark Lich Prince (Book 1)

The Court of Wolves Series

Blooded (Book 1)

Enclave Boxed Sets

Of Beasts and Beauties

This book is for...

Alisha Klapheke, Alistair North, Andrea Peel, Anthony Holabird, Ashley Martinez, Barbara Harrison, Charity Chimni, Charley Curry, Chloe Bratt-Lewis, Clare Sager, Cyndy Shubert-Jett, Dana S. Jackson Lange, Darlene Kunst Rooney, Deb Barringer, Deborah Dunson, Donna Adamek, Donna Levett, Donna Swenson, Emily Allen West, Emily Wiebe, Erin McDonough, Erin Miller, Eugenia Kollia, Fanny Comas, Fiona Andrew, J.M. Butler, Jackie Tansky, Janel Iverson, Jennifer Hoblitt Kaser, Jennifer Moriarity, Jennifer Robertson, Judith Cohen, Karen Borges, Katherine Bennet, Kathy Brown, Kelly Scott, Kimberly, Kris Walls, Kristen White, Krys Baxter-Ragsdale, Lea Vickery, Linda Adams, Linda Levine, Linda Romer, Lyn Andreasen, Maggie Borges, Marilyn Smith, Marla Ramsey, Mary Nguyen, Michelle Ferreira, Nicole Page, Patrycja Pakula, Rachel Cass, Roger Fauble, Samantha Mikals, Scarolet Ellis, Seraphia Sparks, Shannon Childress, Shauna Joesten, Shelby Palmer, Shivani Kitson, Spring Runyon, Susanne Huxhorn, Tanya Wheeler, Teri Ruscak, Tina Carter, Tony Sommer, Tricia Wright, Vicki Michelle, Wanda Wozniczka...

...and everyone else who's supported us and spread the word about our books from the start. We couldn't do this without you, and you being in our corner has meant the world to us.

FALL OF THE REAPER

To Jessica,
without whom this story
never could have been told.

CONTENTS

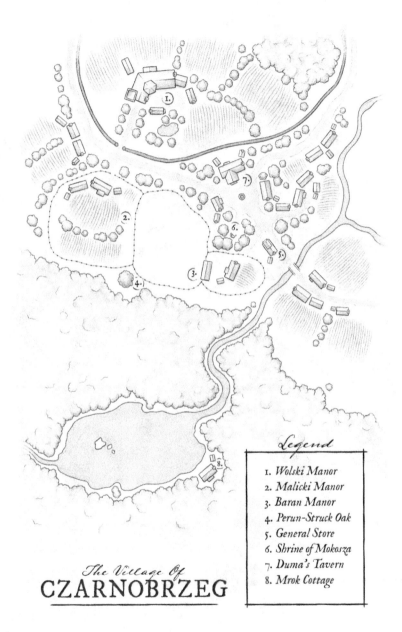

Legend

1. *Wolski Manor*
2. *Malicki Manor*
3. *Baran Manor*
4. *Perun-Struck Oak*
5. *General Store*
6. *Shrine of Mokosza*
7. *Duma's Tavern*
8. *Mrok Cottage*

The Village Of

CZARNOBRZEG

I feel the nights stretching away
  thousands long behind the days
  till they reach the darkness where
  all of me is ancestor.

            — ANNIE FINCH, "SAMHAIN" (1997)

CHAPTER 1

Dark whispers hissed secrets, slithering up Brygida's arm and to her ear like serpents. *There is another*, they whispered. *Another has arrived.*

Yet another. With a grimace, she set aside the pestle and bagged the red raspberry leaf, lemon balm, and chamomile tea for her latest patient, then removed her apron and rolled down her sleeves.

The black crescent mark on her palm throbbed, its darkness and whispers seeping from her skin like smoke. She curled a fist, a tight one, and strode across Anita's small cottage to her altar, where the Scythe of the Mother rested on its two hooks. With a frustrated huff, she retrieved it.

Standing there before the altar, she listened—really

listened—tightening her grip on the scythe's snathe, closing her eyes. *Speak to me.*

Maybe this time she would feel something, anything...

But in her hand, there was nothing but dead wood and silence. The voices of Anita's ancestors had not spoken to her, not yet, but she hadn't given up hope. Maybe one more demon tamed would be enough. Maybe today she would calm the forest back to slumbering at last.

Outside, the sun had risen just beyond the tree line, and long shadows wove over the clearing between the cottage and the forest. Her patient would be here at midday, so she'd need to make this quick.

Crouched in the shade, Matoha waited for her, his red eyes gleaming. His body was goat like, but that was where any semblance of natural appearance ended; he had a ridge of spiky fur down his spine, bladed claw-like legs, and a long black tail, shifting ruminatively. He was always waiting, always watching her. As she approached the oaks, he rose to his full height, his menacing long horns scraping against low-hanging branches.

"Back again?" she asked him.

Matoha opened his mouth, baring rows of pointed teeth in a fearsome grin. *We have a new arrival,* he spoke into her mind.

"So I've heard." She rested her hand against the

trunk of a nearby oak, closing her eyes as she tried to listen for the voices of the wood. But all she could hear was the hiss of demons, those that watched from the shadows. Those that never quite left her for long.

I can take you to it, Matoha prompted. It was tempting to let him take the lead, guide her to the demon, but if she was ever going to reconnect with the forest, to truly heal it, she had to do this herself.

Hefting up her scythe, she gave a short shake of her head before venturing into the forest. Thank Mokosza, Mama had taught her how to track, and recent spring showers had left the ground muddy. Deep imprints in the mud led to the heart of the forest, and she followed them, Matoha accompanying her at a distance.

The canopy of trees had only just begun to fill out, and shafts of light pierced through, illuminating the soft forest floor, where fresh green stalks of ferns poked through dark soil. Months had passed since she'd made her home here, and although she'd defeated every demon that had arrived on these lands, they never stopped and the forest was still restless. She might not be able to hear its voice, but she could feel it as the hairs on the back of her neck stood on end.

A tree branch snapped behind her.

She spun.

A bristly thick-horned creature threw its head back, roaring. Long claws and a cow's tail—a *lichyj*.

It rushed toward her.

Her hand fumbled for the vial of lake water around her neck, but the words of the incantation dried on her tongue. She couldn't use the wrath of the blood.

Leaping out of the way, she rolled into the new ferns. The lichyj skidded to a stop and turned, clawing at the ground, ready to charge once more. This was no lone little *panek*, but a true danger. And she'd made a foolish mistake, relying on instinct.

The crescent mark on her palm throbbed, the faintest trail of darkness seeping from it.

She held up her hand, summoning the power within the mark. Darkness billowed out, like thick black smoke spreading outward and toward the lichyj.

As it reared up, looming over her, their eyes met. With flared nostrils, it inhaled the black smoke and froze in place.

It was hers to command now.

As she held her hand up, it awaited her command, like a part of her. And with a downward motion, it lay down on the ground, eyes trained on her.

That was close, Matoha remarked.

She ignored his commentary; it was never helpful. Matoha had to know how to soothe the forest—why else had he been hovering around her for weeks?—but he had refused to answer her, despite numerous attempts to extract answers. She'd read Anita's grimoire from cover to cover, given numerous offerings to demons and to Holy Mokosza, but no matter what she did, her water powers wouldn't return.

Matoha raised his head, goat ears angling back and forth. The lichyj, too, lifted its head back in the direction of the cottage. *It's a human,* its rumble of a voice announced in her head. *A human. A human has arrived. A human's come to your domain.*

She balled her marked hand into a fist again. *It's not my domain,* she wanted to scream back, but it never changed their minds. The demons understood only one thing: power. But their warnings—that a human was here—meant that her patient, Jadwiga, had likely come to retrieve her morning-sickness tea. Just in time, too. The witchlands were cleansed of chaotic demons, something all the more important with an expectant mother traveling to her cottage.

I await your call, the lichyj said, before it dissipated into the forest, a phantom once more.

Matoha pranced ahead of her, leaping through the forest, avoiding the occasional spots of sunlight. It wasn't like him to stick around after a demon had been subdued. Was something amiss at the cottage?

Hastening her step, she arrived at the forest edge. Instead of finding Jadwiga, as she expected, a man with golden hair waited at the door. Wrapped in a well-tailored and luxurious poppy-red jacket and gleaming brown boots, he cut a lean but strong figure.

Kaspian?

He turned, and what she'd mistaken as golden hair beneath the bright afternoon sun was in fact a darker blond. Not Kaspian. And not Jadwiga either, but her husband, Nikodem, the future lord of Granat.

Shading his hands against the sun, he stared in her direction. Had something happened to Jadwiga? Had she gone into labor early? It was unusual for a first pregnancy but not unheard of.

There is only one reason a man comes to a witch's cottage, and you still have no successor, Matoha remarked.

Snapping her gaze in Matoha's direction, she flushed at the insinuation. *You dare, goat-demon?*

An entertained chuckle lilted to the corners of her mind, echoing.

He'd never attacked her, nor anyone, and didn't give an aura of ill intent, so she'd never tried to tame him... Although now, it was tempting.

Nikodem was a married man, and his wife was her patient. And as Matoha well knew, there would be no successor for her. These were not her witchlands, and until she redeemed herself in the eyes of Mokosza, and for herself, there was no room in her heart for anyone else.

After Kaspian, she wasn't sure she even wanted anyone else. That had gone about as swimmingly as a rock in the Skawa River. She left Matoha at the edge of the forest and jogged over to greet Nikodem. "What brings you here? Is Jadwiga well?"

His mouth dropped open, but he quickly closed it. "Yes, she's well."

If Jadwiga wasn't ill, then perhaps this was just a visit? Nikodem and his sister, Urszula, came here from time to time to share news and keep her company. They didn't say as much, but their regularity had washed away any doubt. Besides, it would be rude not to serve tea now, when he'd come all this way. "Will you come in while I finish Jadwiga's morning-sickness herbs?"

He nodded his head in response.

She led him inside, offered him a plate of rabbit sausage and freshly baked bread, and put the kettle on the fire, the same way Mamusia had always done. The feeling of homesickness was like a punch to the gut, strong but quickly stifled, to reflect on when she was alone.

While the water started to boil, she cleared the table of her mortar and pestle, the herbs, and the other things she had been preparing for Jadwiga. She put them into a jar to give to Nikodem.

Jadwiga's constant morning sickness, even this late in the pregnancy, worried her. She could hardly keep anything down, and when the baby came, she would need her strength.

"Was Jadwiga too tired to make the journey herself?" Brygida asked as she worked. It would not be entirely surprising, given the lateness of her pregnancy. A good husband like Nikodem would gladly make the trip, but she hoped it wasn't something more serious.

"No." Nikodem sat at the table, hands folded in front of him, as he surveyed the cottage. The kettle started to whistle, and Brygida filled a cup and set one before him. He looked deeply into it as the tendrils of steam rose, a slight frown on his brow.

He was a man of few words, and when he visited, he usually just brought some provisions from town, did some work on the cottage or the barn, and listened to her talk. But he'd only just come two days ago. Surely he hadn't come all this way again so soon just to drink tea with her.

"Something on your mind?" she prompted gently.

"There is." He sighed, his shoulders tight and raised toward his neck.

"If there is something wrong with Jadwiga, tell me straight away. I can go to her if necessary."

He shook his head. "She is well."

"Then what's troubling you?" Clearly, something was.

He cleared his throat. "I came because I need your help."

She drummed her fingers on the table, trying to hide her curiosity.

Nikodem met her eyes and held her gaze, as grave as a ghost. "A man calling himself the Prophet of Weles has arrived and is recruiting people to join the Cult of Weles."

Her fingers froze in their drumming. The cult was back? "I thought you and your sister chased the cult out of Granat."

"We did, but he has an ally here, a vassal of my father's, who is protecting him. A wealthy man is housing him. We cannot risk physically removing him without endangering the people of Granat. This vassal would use our intervention as an excuse to start a war with my father."

The crescent on her palm throbbed. The last time she'd gone up against the Cult of Weles, she'd still had Mokosza's favor, and even that hadn't been enough. It had been the blackmark that had killed them. She couldn't risk it, not again.

"I'm sorry, but I can't help you." She stood, pushed in her chair, and stepped behind it.

Nikodem stood as well. "You have the power to stop them, the Mark of Weles." He gestured toward her palm.

She concealed the mark with her other hand. "I know how the Cult of Weles works. They use women to defend themselves against witches. I won't hurt a woman. It goes against everything I believe in."

He took a slow step forward, reaching out to touch her arm, then let his hand fall. "I would not ask you if we were not desperate."

Brygida regarded him with caution and curiosity, her fingers curled over the cursed mark. Normally solemn and quiet, he had to be truly afraid of this Prophet of Weles to make such an emotional appeal to her.

Perhaps there was a way she could defeat this Prophet of Weles that didn't involve killing? After all, she'd found ways to soothe the forest without Mokosza's favor. The people of Granat knew her, and they were starting to trust her; maybe she could find a way to turn their feelings against this prophet before it was too late, before all turned to violence. They needed a time and place for the truth to defeat this so-called prophet.

She inhaled deeply. "I won't harm any women, but I will help you. I think I know just how."

CHAPTER 2

The sun beat down on Kaspian from the bright cloudless sky. He pulled at his collar as sweat dripped down his brow, blurring into his eyes. The effigy of Marzanna, crafted from bundles of dried twigs and wearing an old cornflower-blue dress of Mama's, looked nothing like the goddess of winter he'd seen depicted in tapestries. As a boy, the same effigy had scared him when he'd stood here with Tata, but now his concerns didn't brush fear of the divine so much as the mundane.

The morning was wearing on, and only half the village had arrived.

"Why don't we wait a little longer?" Mama whispered.

"Not a very good turnout," Stryjek remarked, shaking his head. He had stayed longer than they'd anticipated; Kaspian had assumed his uncle would move on to his next destination with the first melt, perhaps never to be seen again. But even now he showed no signs of leaving. He'd become a fixture—a gruff, sardonic one.

Peasants shuffled their feet, few looking toward him, Mama, or Stryjek. This year's drowning of Marzanna was a more subdued affair than most. Usually the return of spring brought with it joy and laughter. But unlike years past, where Tata had overseen the ritual, the peasants seemed more dispirited than usual.

Small wonder. His rulership felt like when he'd worn Tata's boots as a boy, big and hard to fill, and at any moment presaging a fall.

But just as he had grown into Tata's boots, he would grow into his new role as well. With time, he felt confident the people would come to love and respect him.

The loss of Tata and many others had cast a long shadow over the village. They were in need of healing, a return to hope and goodness. Mama had said over and over that his first ritual would set the tone of his rule. What that tone was, he had spent much time debating. Tata had ruled with an iron fist; Kaspian had been practicing what he would say for days, and trying to emulate Tata's tone and delivery, but the words still stumbled on his tongue, like his boyish feet had in those too-big boots. He'd seen Tata perform it every year, for as long as he could remember. But standing here, it was as if all those memories were just too far beyond his grasp, and he was left staring blankly.

Mama nudged him gently. "Perhaps we should get started after all?" she asked brightly.

Was he that transparent? Blinking away his thoughts with a sigh, he cleared his throat and took a step forward. Maybe trying to act like Tata wasn't the best course of action. He should be more himself. "Let us begin..."

He clapped his hands together, stalling for time. "The long winter has passed and... now we welcome the rebirth of spring." He gestured toward the effigy of Marzanna.

Someone coughed, but otherwise there was silence. They stared at him, their reactions more subdued than he would have hoped. But no matter, best to just carry on with the ceremony. It would get better with time; it was only his first after all.

Kaspian gestured to Stryjek, who took his cue, taking up the torch. He tossed it at the effigy, and soaked in oil, it caught fire almost immediately.

As the flames burst to life, Kaspian leaped backward, evading a plume of fire. The peasants gave excited gasps as it burned. Now that they were in the rhythm of things, it felt more natural. And after a few minutes, the fire had faded enough that he could pick up the effigy and carry it. As he got close, the flames licked toward his face, and he had to resist the urge to shield himself from the fire.

Tata had always carried the burning effigy without hesitation, leading the people of the village through the ritual.

Before he could second-guess himself, he grasped the unburnt bottom half and hoisted it up into the air, then took a step toward the Skawa River where it would be tossed.

Mama and Stryjek fell into place behind him as he led the procession down the winding dirt road from the manor and to the river, which cut through their village.

As they walked, the villagers began to sing. *"Marzanna, Marzanna, swim across the seas. Let flowers bloom, and fields turn green..."*

As their procession made its way through the village, shadows stretched on the ground in front of him, and for a moment it was as if he and Tata were walking side by side.

A few more peasants joined their procession, and the more that joined, the livelier they became, their song more joyful in the spirit of the spring celebration. This was the tone he wanted to set for his rule, one of celebration and community.

They reached the banks of the river, near to bursting as the winter snow had melted and filled it with cold, clear water.

The Skawa gurgled happily, and as he stood at its

banks, he remembered Tata standing in this place just a year ago. He'd been so healthy and strong. Who would have thought that in the next year, he would be gone?

But there was no more time for grieving, and the wheel of time moved ever forward. He couldn't continue to look back, only forward. He was the leader now, as Tata had wished, and the village was in his care. To the gods who bore witness, let this be his offering that he would be a good ruler, a fair ruler.

"Now we lay to rest the remnants of winter. Let our crops be plentiful, and our calves and lambs healthy. So I pray to the gods above," Kaspian said, willing it to truth with every fiber of his being.

The villagers' song carried on the wind as they linked hands, along the river bank. Seeing them united this way made his heart swell. He tossed the effigy into the water. The flames were extinguished, and the current swept it out of sight. With it, he washed away his past. It was time to start over fresh. And although he knew it was best to let it all go, he couldn't escape the feeling of longing for what he was leaving behind.

With the ceremony over, Kaspian turned to the peasants. "Let us celebrate the new birth of spring. A feast has been prepared at the manor."

The peasants gave a cheer, and their procession looped back toward the manor house, everyone chattering amongst themselves. The change in their reaction was reassuring. Although there might be growing pains, together they could build a bright future. He was confident of that. But still, he lingered behind, across the river. Together...

The Madwood was beginning to come alive once more, fresh green buds ready to unfurl. Was it spring-time where Brygida was now? Was she walking amongst the trees, communing with nature, free and unburdened? The forest offered no answer.

He likely would never know. Like the effigy of Marzanna, their time together had been swept away and would never return. And yet what memories remained wouldn't depart with the current.

He could say they haunted him. But could a man ever be haunted by something he loved so much? Perhaps enchanted. Or more aptly, bewitched.

He shook his head, hoping to clear it, and took a deep breath before he turned his back on the forest and joined his people. One farmer lagged behind, watching him approach. He was a grizzled old man with white hair and a back starting to bend from years tilling the soil. The frown was not a good sign. Kaspian braced himself.

"My lord," the farmer said, bobbing his head to Kaspian. "I'm sorry to trouble you, but there's a catastrophe. Several farms have been taken by the blight."

The *blight*. The word sent a chill down his spine. The spring planting had started early this year, as the snow had receded earlier than years past, and the farmers had anticipated a bountiful harvest. But a blight, if left unchecked, could sweep through the entire community and leave many starving and hungry.

Mama and Stryjek would know what to do, how to handle a situation like this. If this was his new start, then he needed to take responsibility. The two of them were heading back to the manor, but he was still here. And he was responsible.

"Show me." Kaspian gripped the farmer's shoulder, in what he hoped would be seen as authoritative but kind, and motioned toward the fields.

They hurried down the road, past farmlands with rows upon rows of neat lines of wheat. Small green leaves burst through the fertile soil and swayed in the wind. But as they approached the farmer's land, the field was covered in sickly dead plants, leaves curling inward. Kaspian knelt down and grasped the leaf, which broke off from the stem. What could have caused this?

"That's not all, my lord. My neighbors to the west have been affected as well." The farmer wrung his hat in his hands.

More? If this was widespread, it could cause a panic. Taking the farmer's lead, he visited two more farms, each of them with similar crops dying before they'd ever had a chance to bloom. But what was most unusual was that whatever had caused this blight, it was nothing he'd ever seen before. There was no scale, no signs of disease. Just crops that had withered for no apparent reason.

The farmer yelped and pointed toward the forest. "What is that?"

A shadowy figure moved among the trees, and Kaspian reached for the sword at his belt. Uneasiness settled in his chest. It couldn't be one of the demons, could it?

The figure emerged; it wasn't a demon at all but Stefan, who approached with a sheepish wave, his roughspun work shirt and breeches disheveled.

"What is he doing in the Madwood?" The farmer pointed an accusatory finger at Stefan.

A very good question, and one he himself wanted to know the answer to. Albeit less desperately than the farmer, from what he could tell.

"Where have you been?" Kaspian asked him.

Stefan shrugged. "A horse got loose and ran into the Madwood, I chased after it, but when I did, I got turned around."

A likely story. Especially with no horse at his side.

Kaspian shook his head. Only Stefan would be so reckless as to venture into the Madwood alone. He hadn't set foot there since Brygida had left...

His chest and shoulders tightened, that painful ache of loss surging through him as he recalled her ferocity, beauty, and tenacity. But best not to think about that right now. Best not to think of the woman he'd loved and lost. Best not to think of the most stunning woman he had ever beheld.

"I've seen you going in and out of the Madwood before." The farmer narrowed his eyes, looking at Stefan.

The farmer's rough voice jarred Kaspian from the tumultuous hold of his thoughts.

Stefan pointed at his own chest. "Me? Why would I go into the Madwood? There are *plenty* of other places I'd rather go. You must be mistaken." Stefan laughed off the notion with a dismissive wave, his expression incredulous.

He trusted Stefan, but this disappearing act had become more common lately, even during the ceremony today.

But Stefan would tell him why he was going into the forest when he was ready. And maybe when a terrified farmer wasn't pointing a trembling, accusatory finger at him.

For now, he needed to redirect the farmer's attention. "Are there any other farms affected, um...?"

"Norbert." The farmer looked away from Stefan. "Several. I can show you if you want, my lord?"

He would be missing out on the feast at the manor, but investigating the blight was more important than anything else. "Yes, let's go."

Together, they visited farm after farm. By the eighth, his eyes were hurting, but he was still no closer to the cause of the blight. Many farms had been affected, but thank Perun, not all the farms in the region seemed to have been hit. Those that were had only one thing in common: they were all bordering the Madwood. What could it mean?

As the latest farmer, an elderly rotund man named Wacek, grumbled nearby, Kaspian rubbed his temples and looked to the forest. Was it possible something had come from there to affect the crops?

"Did you see anything in there?" he asked Stefan.

"Trees?" Stefan offered, and Kaspian rolled his eyes.

"What are you going to do, my lord?" Norbert asked.

"We will do everything we can to ensure you and your family are taken care of," Kaspian said.

Wacek stomped up to them. "Why would we trust you? This damned blight is all your fault."

"Wacek, think clearly," Norbert said to him. "This is Łukasz's son, whose face you've seen covered in mud, playing with our children. The blight is terrible, but it's not a man's fault. It's bad luck."

Wacek scoffed, angrily waving Norbert away.

"You think Lord Kaspian can, what, wave a hand and kill your crops?" Stefan asked, eyebrows raised.

"I assure you, I have no control over plants," Kaspian added, doing his best to keep the dryness from his voice. Accusations like this were truly ridiculous, but he wouldn't improve his reputation by mocking his people. The least he could do was to treat them with respect, whether for the sake of affection or order, and hope to be repaid in kind.

"You should have paid for your crimes. That innocent girl died at your hands and now Mokosza has forsaken us all!" The man jutted a finger at Kaspian.

Kaspian's eyes were wide as he stared at the man. The whispers had followed him since Roksana's death, but he'd thought they were just that, rumors. Rumors followed rulers; it was one of the unfortunate aspects of his duty. But never before had someone had the audacity to say that to his face.

"That's enough," Stefan grumbled, rolling up his sleeves as he approached Wacek, but Kaspian held up a hand to stop him.

"I would never have harmed Roksana. The real killer was punished, as you well know," Kaspian replied, squaring his shoulders. Stefan's support was always welcome, but his temper was shorter than it had ever been.

"If it really had been Julian, then this wouldn't be happening," Wacek snarled, his jowls jiggling.

"It *was* Julian, you fool!" Stefan remarked, his brow creased. "I saw it myself. He tried to kill the witch because she figured out it was him! The rusałki let Kaspian go and claimed Julian. You think Iga Mrok and Mokosza herself are corrupt? Does the goddess come here onto your farm and spit on your crops as well, you fool?"

As impassioned as he'd ever seen Stefan, and then some. They'd have to talk soon about what was bothering him—something clearly was.

Wacek crossed his meaty arms, huffing under his breath.

The truth didn't matter to the wronged, angry people looking for a scapegoat. He could stand here arguing with this man that the sky was blue, and their argument would never end if his opponent's ego needed it to be green. He wouldn't squabble with his own villagers. He was lord, and it was time he started acting like it.

"Mokosza already passed judgment, and if you wish to appeal it, go to the rusałki." Kaspian stood up straighter. "I'm here to stop the blight from spreading, and to help those affected as best I can."

"We don't need a murderer's help," Wacek said.

Stefan lunged at the man and grabbed him by the arm. "You will pay for your disrespect. A night in the stocks should be sufficient." Stefan looked back over his shoulder for confirmation. All three faces turned to him.

He could walk away, give an old man mercy. But as Mama had said, now was the time to set the tone of his rule. Tata would never have brooked such disrespect. Kaspian nodded to Stefan, who dragged the man toward the village square.

Wacek wrestled against Stefan, and Norbert stepped in to help subdue him, even as frail as he seemed.

"That which opens can also close," Norbert mumbled with a shake of his head. "You never did learn that, Wacek."

"You dogs, licking the lord's boot!" Wacek spat, spittle flying from his plump lips. "You'll help him bring ruin to us all. Mark my words, Weles will punish you for your crimes!"

Stefan dragged the man away, but his presence lingered, and so did Kaspian. He thought the rumors were just talk. But this went beyond general malcontent. If such acts of disobedience spread, then his rule could be in danger. If the worst happened, all of Rubin would become unstable.

"What should we do about the blight, my lord?" Norbert asked him, while Stefan frogmarched Wacek toward the square alone. Normally handling a man of Wacek's weight would have been a two-man job, but Stefan had not only been quicker to anger lately, but he was stronger, too. Perhaps he'd been working more.

As for the blight, if it spread farther, they would need to go to the witches, but for now the best course of action was to contain the source. "I will provide you with anything you need. The infected fields—we must burn them all. We cannot risk it spreading."

Nor the rumors. But he'd need more than fire to destroy those.

CHAPTER 3

Brygida pulled up the sleeve of a too-large fancy dress as she stepped out from behind the screen. Pulling down the shoulders made the front dip dangerously low. The shoulder width alone must have been made for a woman twice as broad as Brygida.

Dressed in a carmine velvet gown, Urszula leaned back in a chair, tossing a knife in the air and catching it idly. She looked about as comfortable in that gown as a *żbik* wildcat in the cold Skawa River. Across from her, Jadwiga watched, her mouth parted slightly and her eyes following the path of the knife up and down, one hand resting against the swell of her stomach.

Brygida wrapped her arms around her torso, awkwardly trying to keep herself from exposing her body. "What do you think?" she asked uncertainly.

"Oh.... it's...." Jadwiga began cautiously, looking around the room as if for help.

"That's not quite a right fit," Urszula replied with a quick glance in Brygida's direction.

This dress was one of Urszula's; of course it wouldn't fit. She was a head taller and much more muscular than Brygida—the clothes were never going to fit right. But all of Jadwiga's clothes from prior to her pregnancy were too small.

"Do I have to wear a gown to the party?" Not long ago, she'd dreamed of wearing a village woman's dress and attending a feast. But this was not how she'd pictured it, in a sagging borrowed dress, trying to keep her chest covered.

"Believe me, they won't let you attend in trousers, I've tried." Urszula stabbed her knife into the table, which showed many of the same sort of marks.

"Maybe if we tightened the back?" Jadwiga eyed the knife embedded in the table before standing up with a bright smile. "May I?" she asked Brygida.

Brygida nodded in response as Jadwiga circled her, pulling at the dress and humming under her breath in a way that could be seen as good and bad. "It's a little long, but I think we can make it work."

She tugged behind Brygida for a few moments, cinching in the waist of her dress and keeping the front from flapping open and exposing her breasts. The sleeves were still a little too big and the hem dragged on the ground, but at least she would be decent.

Jadwiga stood back, her hand once again resting on her round belly. "There, you look lovely."

"Are you sure you're all right with me attending this party with Nikodem?" Brygida prompted. In her experience, when a witch was near, most women held their husbands a little closer. She would never harm a married man, as long as he was good and didn't offend Mokosza, but the women who'd wed them certainly seemed to think witches desired to murder them with impunity. Or perhaps it had to do with how unmarried witches without husbands managed to bear their daughters.

Jadwiga flapped her hand at her. "Of course. Nikodem and I have an understanding with one another, and besides, I'm much too tired lately with the baby coming soon. It's better I stay home." She shared a furtive look with Urszula that was difficult to decipher.

An understanding? What did they understand?

Nikodem had visited the cottage before, so perhaps Jadwiga understood he wouldn't be murdered with impunity. Or... "managed" for the sake of bearing a daughter.

If Jadwiga was all right with it, then she shouldn't be making too much of a fuss about it. Besides, she needed to handle the so-called Prophet of Weles, and that meant gaining entry to an elite gathering. Nikodem would be her key.

After a word of thanks to Jadwiga, Brygida went downstairs with Urszula, where Nikodem spoke with a man, laughing.

Laughing? Since she'd come to Granat, she'd never seen Nikodem laugh, but now, his eyes lit up. The other man, well built with black curls of shoulder-length hair, touched Nikodem's hand in an affectionate way, their gazes meeting.

She'd seen that look before; it was the same way Mama looked at Mamusia...

Was that why Jadwiga hadn't objected to Brygida being his guest? Perhaps this was their "understanding"?

Jadwiga had given no indication that it bothered her, sharing the one she loved with another. Or it might be something else. Jadwiga was a lord's daughter, and Nikodem, after all, was the heir to Granat's lordship... Kaspian had been so bound up by his duties. Had Jadwiga and Nikodem found a way to fulfill their duties and still follow their hearts? Did Jadwiga have a lover as well? Then there could be hope that—

"Are we ready?" Urszula shifted in her velvet gown with a quiet tearing sound as threads strained against fabric.

The two men turned as she and Urszula entered,

and the handsome stranger bowed as they approached. "Ladies, you both look ravishing this evening."

"Promises, promises." Urszula rolled her eyes. "Ravish me, then, Anatol Bilski."

"Come now, set your sights higher, Urszula," Anatol jested. "You could do far better than me." Turning to Brygida, Anatol bowed and took her hand. "I find myself at a loss, lady. You know my name, but I have yet to learn yours."

The intensity of his pale-green gaze made her heart beat faster. She bobbed her head. "Brygida Mrok."

It had been months since she'd claimed her family name. It felt wrong somehow to say it aloud.

"Niko, how have you been hiding such a charming beauty from me all this time?" Anatol playfully hit Nikodem's upper arm.

Nikodem ignored his jibing. "Ready?"

Brygida nodded an affirmative, stuffing down the feelings of homesickness that threatened to bubble out of her. Tonight she needed to focus on the task at hand.

The group left the manor house together, with Anatol doing the talking for all of them.

"I'm glad you were willing to help us, Brygida," Anatol said in the carriage. "My father has been insufferable with these cultists. He won't hear a word I have to say against them. And now this so-called 'prophet'? He's, well, you'll see what I mean when we get there."

She nodded along, her throat dry. They arrived at

the Bilski manor house, where a crowd had gathered and raised voices could be heard from within. She wasn't here to socialize, but some small part of her eagerly anticipated the rare sights: pearl buttons on fine dresses, jewels on fingers and ears, elaborate dances and fancy dishes... Things she'd thought she'd wanted. All of that felt hollow now compared to losing everyone she loved.

Nikodem offered his bent arm, and she grasped it before they entered a lavishly adorned foyer, with walls of granite and archways made of stained oak logs, with vases and garlands of poppies. Bright red with dark centers, they were often the first wildflowers to blossom on burnt fields. On battlefields besieged by mud, where nothing would grow, it was poppies that sprouted from the memories of dead men. A reminder.

Thank you. I take your caution, blooms of remembrance. She had to succeed tonight. The last thing she wanted was to ever see a battlefield of the dead come from this man's lies.

Taking a deep, cleansing breath, she proceeded into the main hall. She'd only ever seen two others, that of the Wolski and Grobowski manors. Although this one was less spacious than both, it was full to bursting. A cluster of finely garbed people gathered around a tall figure standing with his hands on his hips. But even with his back to her, a charismatic and easy confidence seeped from him as he cocked his head to one side as if to better hear a joke. The golden hair struck an even stronger chord within her. Kaspian? Would he be here?

No, she was just seeing things because this place reminded her of his home. Her mind wandered to the wintry night of Kolęda, when she'd last visited him there. For a fleeting moment, it had been dazzling— before the realities had set in, and then, the disaster at the hearth...

"That's the bastard?" Urszula growled, jutting her chin out in the golden-haired man's direction.

"Indeed it is," said Anatol.

With an effortless grace, Nikodem led her through the crowd, his gait as confident as his smiles and niceties were forced. She'd never seen him like this, but as she'd learned at the Wolski manor, a political life sometimes required donning a mask. Lady Rubin had been a master of that.

A ring of women surrounded the prophet—no, the Dog of Weles—whose handsome face nearly shone as he spoke to them, his hands weaving in grand gestures. He was perfectly coiffed, dressed in finely tailored clothes glittering with embroidery. "When we moved away from Szmaragd last fall, their harvest was thrice what it had been in previous years. It was all thanks to Weles's favor."

"Praise the darkness!" the women surrounding him replied as one. All of them wore the same black, high-necked gowns with innumerable buttons down the back and a horned-snake pin on their chests.

These had to be the inquisitors she'd heard about. Were there any among them who'd had a hand in Anita's death? Her hand tightened into a fist, and the Mark of Weles on her palm throbbed.

"The way I heard it, that region has been suffering a famine," Urszula interjected.

The man's blue eyes flickered toward Urszula, and he plastered a smile on his face, one that didn't reach his eyes. "Seeking attention, especially with lies, is the mark of a witch, girl."

The room went silent.

Urszula planted her hands on her hips. "I am no mere 'girl.' 'Girls' are children. I am a full-grown woman, the daughter of Lord Granat, and I will have you treat me with the respect that I deserve."

He shook his head. "This is what I've been saying. Women cannot be trusted to tell the truth, because we cannot know who amongst them are witches simply seeking attention. That is why service is their proper place. It is only under the guidance of one who hears the voices of the gods that women can find true purpose. Not seeking attention or flaunting their bodies." He narrowed his gaze at Urszula while his entourage of black-clad inquisitors nodded and whispered their agreement, clustering around him like a field of mud.

"I serve no man." Urszula balled her fist, and only Nikodem's hand on her elbow stopped her from striking, although she gritted her teeth as if she would very much like to rearrange the features of the Dog's face.

Nonetheless, the inquisitors around him shielded him with their bodies. Getting to him would not be easy.

"Remember your place, girl," the Dog of Weles said. "You should not threaten those who are chosen by the dark god."

The crescent shape mark throbbed again. This man was not chosen, that much was certain. And she could stand by no longer.

"You are not His chosen," Brygida declared, as all faces turned to her, "because I am." She held up her hand with the Mark of Weles.

The inquisitors' eyes widened, and almost as one, they pointed at her face. *Mokosza and Weles, please, I beseech you... guide me.*

"Those eyes... Those purple eyes... You bring a witch here! Do you wish for demons to destroy your people and for Weles to condemn this land?" the Dog of Weles shouted.

"It was the cult's interference that brought demons and misfortune to this land," she replied, unyielding.

The gathered guests muttered amongst themselves.

But the inquisitors closed in around her, their eyes bright with that sliver of madness. How could she fight them off if they attacked her? She had Nikodem and Urszula on her side, but they were outnumbered.

"Witches lie. We have all seen the evil of their power, how they corrupt and twist the truth," the Dog of Weles said.

The crowd murmured their agreement. She was losing them. "The Mark of Weles doesn't lie."

"If that's what it is," the Dog crooned. "But it's just another falsity, another way your kind tries to deceive good people."

She clutched her hand. She could call on her power, destroy him here and now, and take vengeance for those he had killed. But even if she only harmed him, then she'd be the evil he claimed her to be, or worse a murderer, when this was a war of ideas.

Nikodem grabbed Brygida by the chin and brought her close, his lips just barely grazing hers.

There was a collective gasp from the crowd... and perhaps one from her.

"Our region is free of demons, thanks to Brygida's efforts," Nikodem said in an authoritative voice to the crowd.

All eyes turned toward her. Their almost-kiss had been a declaration: Granat stood on the side of the witches. It was just the thing she'd needed. "I am the true chosen of Weles, and I can prove it."

She held up her hand once more, willing the

tension there free, like a wolf from its den. *I beg you, Weles, let no one come to harm.*

The dark smoke began to spill from her mark. It swirled around the room. The inquisitors and the Dog took steps back, their eyes wide.

The smoke took shape, and over the heads of those gathered, a giant black wolf loomed. It opened its maw, and with a hiss, the darkness spread over the inquisitors, like a force pressing them to submission. It was unmistakable—the wolf was a symbol of Weles.

The inquisitors cried out, pointing at it. "The dark god has come!"

Even they could not deny the power.

The smoke-wolf raced around the room, snapping at the inquisitors. They fell backward and then fled from it, leaving behind only the Dog, who stood back with a blanched face. The wolf completed its circle around the room, then stopped at Brygida's side, its dark ethereal body massive beside her.

She couldn't help a tilt of her head and a raised eyebrow at the Dog.

He glared at her, his handsome face twisted into something truly ugly. "You think your tricks are impressive, but the dark god remembers, and you will be punished for your blasphemy." And then with a quick turn, he quit the room, leaving a hush in his wake.

The silence throbbed like a beating heart for several

moments, not a body daring to move nor a voice daring to speak.

At last, Anatol stepped into the center, clapping his hands. "Well, well, wasn't that exciting? We hope our little display hasn't ruined your evening. Please drink and be merry."

The murmur of conversation returned, and Brygida hurried out of the main hall into an adjoining room. Her heart raced, and she couldn't stop the smile from spreading across her face. She'd done it; she'd chased away the Cult of Weles without harming anyone. It was a small victory, but a victory nonetheless.

Still, although the battle had been won, the war was far from over.

"That was impressive." Beside her, Anatol nodded his awe. "Do you do parties?"

"'Impressive'?" A smile ghosted across Urszula's lips. "She practically grabbed him by the eggs and cut 'em from his shaking body!"

Anatol shuddered, wrinkling his nose at Urszula. "Don't ever change, O Treasure of Granat."

Brygida's hands trembled, and her head felt as if it would float from her shoulders.

"You should come back to the manor," Nikodem murmured to her.

She frowned, turning to him in a daze. "Why?"

"Didn't you hear what the prophet said?" Anatol asked. "That whole 'you will be punished' and so on and so forth?" His imitation was spot on... and then some, maybe ten times as severe.

She set her hands on her waist, lifting her chin. It was nothing but empty words. She had shown everyone the truth, and even if he came for her, she could handle him the same way she had today.

"His power is only one of lies, and it crumpled when faced with the truth." And if he tried to fight her with something sharper than lies, although she didn't wish for it to go that far, she had an answer to that, too.

CHAPTER 4

Outside Kaspian's window, the horizon burned red, not with the dying light of day but the ambient glow of burning fields. All told, six farms had been affected by the blight, and every last one of them bordered the Madwood. It could be a coincidence, but something told him there was more to it than that. Whatever had killed these crops was nothing like he'd ever seen before.

"Kaspian, come away from the window," Mama said.

The servants had arrived with tonight's entree, roasted squab in butter with a mushroom gravy, and Mama and Stryjek awaited him at the same worn, oaken table where his whole family had once had dinner together.

Looking at that empty chair at the head of the table, his instinct was to search for Tata, who'd take his place, same as always. These moments were fleeting now, and easing. But in the mood he was tonight, it hit him particularly hard.

Kaspian sat down, and Mama brushed his hand as he did so. "Don't worry about the blight. You made the right decision burning the fields. We're fortunate we caught it early enough in the season. Had the rains come, it could have become a worse problem."

"I need to know what caused it." He couldn't fathom a reason why fields bordering the Madwood would fall to blight. Despite its name, the forest had never been detrimental to the abutting farms. Just a few months ago, he would've broached it with Brygida, discussed theories with her, searched for the answers together. But those months were past. Ewa and Liliana would know what had caused it, but he was less concerned with the "what" and more with the "who."

Mama filled a goblet of wine for herself. "These things are a mystery only the gods know."

It had been months since he'd let a drop of wine pass his lips. He wanted to be clear headed—no more running away. But there were times that he missed that comfortable numbness, longed for the release of oblivion. He couldn't trust himself with it, not yet, not while he welcomed the ghost of Tata at every opportunity.

He tore his gaze away from her goblet and took a long drink of his tea. "Well, it's one mystery I wish the gods would reveal to me. How can I protect my people from a faceless enemy?"

Mama laughed. "There's no enemy. The peasants are resistant to change, but you will win them over, I'm certain of it. Let's put the subject to rest."

"I agree." Stryjek yawned as he swirled his goblet of wine. "All this talk about farming has practically put me to sleep."

Kaspian cut into his squab and popped a bite into his mouth. If only Mama's words could be enough... but she hadn't seen the look in that man's eyes when he had flung his accusations. It had been the look of a madman, who'd truly believed what he was saying. There was no winning over that kind of devotion.

But these rumors had to come from somewhere. And this sort of thing spawned from discontent. Perhaps if he talked with his people, heard their complaints, they would be less likely to revolt.

"I heard a delicious rumor that one of our stable hands and a village widow are having the most salacious affair," Stryjek said, waggling his eyebrows. "Care to know who?"

Kaspian sighed. "Stryjek, really, aren't you too old to be gossiping?"

Stryjek shrugged. "There's not much else to do. I forgot how dreadfully boring it was here." He took a long gulp of his wine.

Boring was good. If Czarnobrzeg was boring, it meant unrest, rebellion, and worse weren't brewing.

Kaspian's gaze trailed back to the window, where the sun had begun to set, and the pinkish-red of the sky was obscured by clouds of smoke. It was rather beautiful if bittersweet; it was times like this that his hands ached to go and paint.

Mama shook her head. "Kaspian, tomorrow can you make time for me in the afternoon? I thought, given the circumstances, a tour of the farms would be wise."

"Mm," he replied, shoveling food in his mouth.

Painting had always cleared his head, helped sort out the jumble of thoughts. But he couldn't just run off to paint a sunset now; he was lord of Rubin. His attention should be on his duty, and nothing else. This was no time for frivolity and selfish indulgence.

Tata would have brooked no rebellion, and would have done much more than put that farmer in the stocks. But he wanted to be the sort of ruler whose people trusted him, not just feared him.

"Well, as riveting as this conversation is, I think I'll see myself to a pub." Stryjek pushed back his chair with a scrape. "Maybe Agata will chase out someone else with her cleaver again." Stryjek finished his wine, then left the pair of them alone.

Mama sighed once he was gone. "Really, if he finds us so terribly boring, I don't know why he bothers to stay."

"The gossip," Kaspian remarked. "Or Agata's cleaver-chasing."

Mama gave him a smile. "There is that."

Servants brought around the dessert. He and Mama had just relaxed into conversation when there was a knock on the door.

Mama frowned. "Come in."

In strode Rafał, the captain of the guard. "My lady, my lord, I am sorry to disturb your supper, but there's been an incident."

A cold chill ran down his spine. He steadied his breathing. "What is it?"

"There was a break-in at the granary."

"A break-in?" Mama asked. "Who would dare steal from us?"

Wacek, the farmer who'd accused him of murder, for one. Perhaps he had friends who were on his side, who didn't like the punishment Kaspian had put upon him. "How much was taken?"

"That's the thing, my lord, it was just seeds and some grain that had been set aside for the affected farmers."

"How strange," Mama said.

Kaspian frowned. He had so many questions. How would anyone have known the amount set aside for the affected farmers? Why take that, when it would already be given? And why not more?

None of the farmers would have stolen what they'd already freely receive.

There was no more denying it now; it was sabotage.

Someone here wanted to dig a grave beneath him, eroding his ability to take care of his people, and perhaps even their ability to feed themselves. If the saboteur caused the blight, this was likely only the beginning. He would need to quash this now before it truly got out of hand.

But who was the mastermind? Dariusz was gone, killed during the attack on Brygida's mothers. Agata made no secret of her dislike of him and his family, but she was more likely to start a mob than to subtly undermine him this way. There were few others in the village with the selfish ambition, the reach, and the cunning to attempt something like this.

Unless the head of this snake wasn't *in* the village, or even Rubin... and he was only seeing its tail here.

Either way, this saboteur had harmed his people, and that would not go unchecked.

He would get to the bottom of this.

***

BRYGIDA'S MIND WAS RACING AS SHE RETURNED TO THE forest. The rush of chasing away the Dog of Weles coursed through her veins. Without violence, she had won her battle, and the victory was sweet. He wouldn't be gone for good, but he was gone for now, and that meant a breath for her, and for everyone.

A full moon illuminated Anita's cottage in the center of the clearing. Dark windows and a dark doorway. She slowed her steps toward the empty cottage, sighing out a lengthy breath. Although she slept there, cooked there, practiced there, it was still only a hut, four walls and a floor and a roof. It had none of what would have made it a home. There was no Mama stoking a fire. No Mamusia humming over her loom to greet her. Just four walls. A floor. A roof.

The cold hit her eyes, and tears stung them. Her heart ached for Mama and Mamusia, but weeping wouldn't change anything.

Outside the cottage was a barrel of rainwater. She walked over to it, splashed cool water onto her face, and took a long, healing breath. There wasn't time to cry. She would make amends as best she could and return to them, no matter what.

The reflection of the moon rippled and twisted on the water's surface, and she raised her hand, focusing all her concentration upon it as she tried to bring the water out of the barrel.

The surface trembled slightly, and for a moment, it looked as if it would slosh over the edge. But before it could, the water stilled as if it had never been touched at all.

She had been closer this time. Maybe facing the

inquisitors and the Cult of Weles wasn't enough. But she was on the right path at least.

"Is anyone at home? We need help!" a voice called from behind her.

At the edge of the clearing, Urszula and an older woman she did not recognize half-carried a stumbling Jadwiga.

Blood stained the front of Jadwiga's nightgown.

Brygida rushed over toward them. "Bring her inside immediately."

Jadwiga moaned in pain as she clutched her bulging belly. It was too early for the baby to come, but if she was bleeding, there was no time to consider it.

Brygida led the women into the house and threw back the blankets on her bed for Jadwiga to lay down upon. Urszula lifted Jadwiga up and rested her on the bed as she writhed in pain.

The stain of blood was growing.

"She's bleeding. That's not good, is it?" Urszula asked.

She'd assisted Mamusia at numerous child beds, had even delivered her first baby this last summer, but she'd had Mamusia's soft words guiding her, and that had been a normal, uncomplicated third-born child.

There was no time for doubt; Jadwiga's life was at risk.

"Build up that fire and put water on to boil," Brygida

said to Urszula, while the older woman stroked Jadwiga's forehead. She groaned again.

The labor pains were close together.

"Jadwiga, you are going to get through this. Don't worry."

"Please," Jadwiga bit out. "Just save my baby." She panted as another spasm contracted her belly.

Brygida rolled back her stained nightgown, and everything below her waist was a bloody mess. Jadwiga was losing too much blood and too fast. If she didn't help her deliver this baby, Jadwiga might bleed to death.

Urszula sparked the flames to life, and Brygida rushed over to her cabinet, grabbing jars. One dropped to the ground, where it shattered to pieces.

She leaned forward on the counter. She had to get it together; a woman's life was at stake here. *Don't panic,* Mamusia's voice came to her. *If you, the midwife, panic, the mother will sense it and make the delivery that much harder.* Taking a few more calming breaths, she selected the herbs for the brew that would reduce the bleeding. She dumped the herbs she needed into her pestle, ground them up, and put them in a cup, into which she poured the water Urszula had boiled for her.

She brought it to the older woman who was at Jadwiga's bedside. Her hair was gray streaked, and there was a look of Jadwiga about her face. Her mother, perhaps.

"Here. Help her drink this." Brygida handed her the cup as she assisted Jadwiga in sitting up. They helped her drink down the remedy.

It would take time to slow the bleeding, and she just hoped it would be enough. Now all they could do was wait. The pains were still too far apart for her to start pushing.

"It was dangerous to bring her here, but with her bleeding, I knew we couldn't wait for you to come to us," said Jadwiga's mother.

"You made the right decision, um...?" Brygida said, more to reassure Jadwiga's mother than out of any confidence she felt in her own ability.

"Ania," Jadwiga's mother replied.

There should have been weeks yet before she'd have to tend to Jadwiga's birth, but now everything Mamusia had taught her was fleeing her grasp.

Busy. She needed to keep her hands busy. Her mind might have forgotten, but her hands would remember. She went over to her shelf filled with rows and rows of medicine—she'd been replacing what had been destroyed when Anita's cottage had burned, but what if she had missed something? What if the bleeding didn't slow? What if the baby would be stillborn? Fear clenched at her throat.

"I'll fetch some water." Brygida walked out of the cottage and back to the barrel.

She submerged her face entirely and screamed into

the water, sending bubbles rising to the top. Calm. Jadwiga had to be surrounded by serenity to help instill that calmness in her, too.

When she came back up, she was panting for breath, and Urszula stood beside her, arms crossed over her chest.

"Have you ever delivered a baby before?" Urszula sized her up dubiously.

"I have." She crossed her arms, too, not liking the look on Urszula's face.

"You can't go into battle without a clear head. Whatever fear or doubt in yourself you're feeling in this moment, leave it outside this door. When you go back in there, Jadwiga needs you to be strong."

It was just the sort of thing she needed to hear. Mama would have said the same thing to her if she were here.

With the sleeve of her nice gown—the one she'd borrowed from Urszula—she wiped the water from her face, then grabbed a bucket from next to the barrel and stepped back inside.

And as Urszula had said, once she stepped through that door, a new clarity of purpose filled her. Jadwiga's face glistened with sweat, and her blood stained the blankets crimson. Unless she could intervene, this woman would die on her bed in blood and agony.

"Gather all the cloth you can and fill this bucket with boiled water," Brygida commanded, and Urszula went to obey. Grabbing a stool, Brygida took her place at the end of the bed to properly examine her patient. The pains had progressed closer together, and she was ready. It was time. "Jadwiga, you are going to meet your baby tonight, and I need you to push for me. Understand?"

Jadwiga nodded to her while clutching Ania's hand hard enough to break it. Urszula brought over the cloth and full bucket, and as the next contraction hit, Jadwiga pushed, her face straining with the effort.

"Good. That was perfect. Now rest," Brygida said soothingly.

Over and over, Jadwiga pushed. Time lost all meaning as she labored into the night. In an ideal world, this was what she and all the Mrok witches before her had been born to do. Not Reaping men who murdered women. Not calming a forest waking due to the violence of men. Not mixing bruise balm to heal a wife's latest badge of brutal marriage. But this. Welcoming new life into the world, and protecting the women who created it.

But this was not an ideal world. Just as she welcomed its new life and protected its women, so too did she have to stand up to its violence and subdue it when necessary. It was precisely that stand which made way for the peace new life needed in order to thrive.

Mamusia had told her that she remembered and loved every baby she'd ever delivered and would do anything for their sake. Jadwiga's baby hadn't even been born yet, but as she awaited its arrival, her heart knew the truth of Mamusia's words. There was nothing she wouldn't do for the sake of this child.

At last, the crown of the baby's head appeared.

They're coming, the demons hissed into her mind.

Two babies? That wasn't right. Brygida's eyes, heavy from the long hours, blinked with a renewed sense of energy. "We're nearly there."

A few more pushes, and with tears from everyone around the room, the baby boy came into the world screaming and covered in blood.

Holding the tiny life in her hands, an indescribable feeling welled up inside her. His tiny red face was scrunched up as he cried, filling his healthy lungs with air. Jadwiga cried, too, as did her mother, and even Urszula 's eyes looked misty.

Brygida wrapped the baby in clean cloth, then brought the child to his mother for the first time. Sweat drenched Jadwiga's face, and dark circles shadowed her eyes, but never had anyone looked so radiant as in that moment, when Jadwiga held her child for the first time.

Had Mamusia felt the same way the first moment she'd held her? Tears slid down Brygida's cheeks as she thought of the life she'd left behind. To hide her tear-streaked face from the others, she gathered up the soiled clothing and the bucket of bloody water she'd washed her hands in.

But as she passed by the cottage window, the flickering of light caught her eye. She frowned as she squinted into the dark.

They're coming, the demons hissed again.

Torches. A crowd of people approached with innumerable torches. Coming right this way.

CHAPTER 5

Kaspian paced the length of the study, tugging at the too-tight collar of his shirt. The men who had broken in and stolen the grain and seeds from the stores had been caught, thanks to Captain Rafał and his men. It had taken less than an evening, and from what Kaspian had heard, they had not tried hard to cover their tracks. In fact, they'd been caught boasting at the Duma Inn.

He swabbed his forehead with a handkerchief. They had all but confessed to their crimes already, and he had a sinking feeling about this trial.

There was a light knock on the door before Mama slipped in. "Everyone is waiting."

"I don't like all the spectacle of this." He had stood before crowds before, but somehow the thought of the dissenters out there, their jeering faces, made the pit of his stomach clench. These saboteurs had been too easily caught, which led him to believe the real mastermind behind them was still unknown and free.

Mama placed a hand on his shoulder. "They dared to steal from the lord of Rubin. If you don't show a strong hand in this matter, then they will only be encouraged to do greater harm. You must be strong for your people."

She was right, but this was all too easy. Punishing them was the right thing to do, but it still felt as if by doing so, he was playing right into their hands somehow. Although he couldn't see what benefit there might be in getting caught and punished for their crimes.

Taking a deep breath, he stood straighter. Whatever game they were playing, he would find a way to outmaneuver them. He had to. "Let's go."

He followed Mama out of the study and into the great hall. The tables and benches had been pushed aside, and a crowd of grim faces filled the space instead, muttering amongst themselves.

At the head of the room, a single chair awaited. Tata had sat here countless times before; twice a year, the community would gather to speak about their grievances and go to Tata for fair judgment. And whenever a crime had been committed, Tata had passed judgment then, too, sometimes in private, and other times at public trials. Tata's wisdom had always seemed so easy, but he must have worked very hard to make it seem so.

Today, he'd have to use his own wits to sort this out. When he had first been named heir, he had studied the laws, and he still had Tata's example to guide him and Mama's advice to lean on, if need be. He would pass fair judgment upon these men.

He held his head high as he strode forward, Mama and Stryjek following after him to the waiting chair at the end of the room. As he approached, most of the crowd inclined their heads. When he reached the chair, his hands trembled; he folded them behind his back.

Staring out at the people here, he knew many— farmers and neighbors, not a faceless mob, but friends and people he'd known his entire life. Good people who'd come to see justice done.

He took a deep breath. "Bring forth the accused."

The guards brought forth the prisoners, two young men—farm hands from Malicki manor, Roksana's family farm. Maciek and Albin. When he'd imagined the culprits breaking into the granary, it had been nameless, faceless others. Strangers. Not men he'd known by name, whom he'd greeted every time he'd passed by Malicki manor. Men who'd been friends of Julian...

Was that it? Even after the revelation that Julian had been a rapist and a murderer—had *killed* Roksana, whom all the village had adored—were his friends still so loyal to Julian that they'd try to take revenge on Rubin? On *him*?

The reasons didn't matter; they had committed a crime, attempting to steal from those in need, and had insulted him, bringing his rulership into question. It was inexcusable. He cleared his throat and licked dry lips. "You stand accused of theft. What do you have to say for your crimes?"

Maciek, the man closest to him, raised his squarish head with a defiant glare. "We did it."

Just so? Kaspian steeled himself as murmurs rippled through the crowd. It wasn't unheard of for criminals to confess their crimes in hopes of lessening their punishment. Perhaps it had been nothing but a drunken night gone wrong, but that defiant glare made him uneasy. "That grain was allotted for those of this community who've been harmed by the blight. Why did you steal what was meant for them?"

Maciek spat on the ground. "I confess only to taking from a wicked man who has no right to rule." Next to him, Albin nodded, skin and bones as he'd always been slender as a fork.

Kaspian shuddered, as if a cold bucket of water had been dumped over his head. Then this had been their plan all along, to use the trial to rally a public outcry against him. But he would not give them a stage to do so.

"How dare you speak to your lord this way," Kaspian said, taking a harsh tone as he gestured briskly to the guards.

"This family is cursed!" Maciek shouted, his square face turning red. "By thwarting Mokosza's justice, you've brought misfortune on us all. We only sought to right the wrongs of the man who got away with the murder of sweet Roksana."

"Silence," Kaspian roared over them. His voice reverberated off the ceiling, echoing back at himself, unfamiliar and sobering.

The people went silent, all eyes upon him. They dared use Roksana in this scheming, in these lies? He breathed heavily, his hands clenched, knuckles white.

"I will say this once and never again. The one who killed Roksana, my betrothed, was Julian, and he paid for his crimes according to Mokosza's justice." He'd said it so many times, his mouth turned to ash to even think of saying it once more. He knew that most of those gathered here did not doubt his innocence. But he wanted to deliver a message to the one who had plotted against him, using vicious lies, and who he suspected was here among the crowd. "Any who wish to continue arguing this truth and spreading malicious lies will face the same consequences as these men."

There was a hushed silence as he finished speaking.

He scanned the crowd, meeting the faces of those assembled. None stood out among them as possible dissenters, but he could feel it, like a foul wind. "These men shall spend two days in the stocks, one day for their theft and one day for their impertinence."

As Maciek and Albin struggled against the guards dragging them from the hall, the silence claiming the crowd broke at last. Whispers brushed from mouth to ear in chaotic strokes, and although the silence had broken, the peace did not.

Grimly, Kaspian followed the guards outside the manor house. He would see the punishment enacted, although he took no pleasure in it. There was a time for compassion, and there was a time for a firm hand. The time for compassion had run out.

The crowd followed them through the village to the square, where the guards put the struggling prisoners into the stocks. The crowd buzzed like an angry swarm, all their malice turned on the two men. Whether it had been his words that had incited them or just a thirst for blood, he couldn't be certain.

But he stood by, watching as villagers passed around rotten produce and tossed it at the pair, who shouted back as the crowd taunted them.

"You are blind to the truth! And you all shall pay!" Maciek yelled, wincing as a parsnip struck his brow.

"It is the witches who have corrupted our village," Albin added, squeezing his eyes shut. "The babes that die in the crib, the crops rotting in the field! Open your eyes!" An egg collided with his temple, and yellow yolk rolled down his cheek. Rotten yolk.

The odor turned Kaspian's stomach, but he would wait here until it was done.

Near the back of the crowd, a chant started to rise, at first difficult to hear, but as it grew closer, the voices rang clear. "Burn! The! Witches! Burn! The! Witches!"

The chanters shoved through the crowd, faces he didn't recognize. They stepped in front of Maciek and Albin in the stocks, some of them pushing those throwing detritus. One of the unknown men elbowed Zofia, who fell to the ground.

Kaspian reached for his blade and pushed into the fray, striking the stranger in the gut with its pommel.

The stranger doubled over, and as he slumped, Kaspian pushed him aside. Morning sunlight glinted off the pin on the stranger's lapel: the horned serpent. The Cult of Weles.

Kaspian slid a step backward, leveling his sword at the cultists.

"Arrest them," he ordered his guards.

They leaped into action, rounding up the remaining troublemakers and then binding their hands.

The cult. The Cult of Weles was here. It had lurked like death over the dying, and at last it had struck. But how many had come? A small force of malcontents, or an enemy army? And how many among his people had been converted?

As the crowd dispersed, Kaspian heaved for breath, staring around the square, his gaze turning to every corner, every face, and every lapel where a horned serpent pin might gleam.

Stefan joined him, his face splattered with what appeared to be rotten produce, which he wiped away with a grim expression. "Nina has terrible aim."

Kaspian blew out a breath, but none of the tension left his shoulders. "One of the men wore a Cult of Weles pin."

"The cult?" Stefan straightened, scrutinizing the few villagers who lingered and chatted amongst themselves. "They're the ones behind this, I bet." He gestured toward the mess that surrounded them.

It made sense. The cultists had to be the ones spreading the rumors as well. If it was a coordinated attack, then what were their goals? To conquer Rubin from within? To sow dissent?

The Cult of Weles had seemed like a strange sect with dark intentions toward witches, but if they were manipulating rumors and attacks in villages, their goals could go far beyond what he'd imagined. And there was no telling what damage they intended to Czarnobrzeg, Rubin, and its people. Not unless he took action.

"I need your help." He turned to Stefan. "We need to find out who is involved and what they want. Are you with me?"

Stefan narrowed his eyes at the square before

looking over to him, a corner of his mouth curling upward. "Do I want to shovel manure or knock some teeth out of these cultists' mouths?" He tilted his head in mock contemplation before punching a fist into his palm. "Let's do this."

CHAPTER 6

Brygida threw open her door and rushed outside as the first torch sailed through the air, landing on her thatched roof.

The dry thatch caught fire and spread quickly. Jadwiga and her newborn son were still within. They were at risk from the fire inside, but they'd be at the mercy of the cultists outside.

Brygida hesitated in the doorway. One way or the other, she'd need help to keep the mother and baby safe." Urszula!"

Outside, women cloaked in black with the white horned serpent on their chests—inquisitors—closed in around her, surrounding the cottage.

She grasped for her vial of lake water, trying to summon the wrath of the blood, but it did not come to her. Not so much as a drop to extinguish the fire.

"You, who have spit on the face of Holy Weles, shall be cleansed by his righteous fire." A tall inquisitor threw a second torch onto her roof. A tendril of smoke rose into the night sky.

Urszula rushed outside, sword drawn. "What is the meaning of this?" she roared, eyes wild.

The inquisitors didn't so much as flinch upon seeing her.

Drawing her sword, the tall leader stepped up to Urszula. "All those who harbor a witch are just as evil as they are! You shall feel the fury of Weles."

Urszula roared, swinging her blade at the leader, who fought her with fire and numbers.

The fire was spreading. She couldn't let Jadwiga and her baby burn. But she couldn't kill these women either. Their voices, the fighting, it all sounded muffled, as if her head were underwater.

Without Mokosza's favor, what could she do? How could she—

A scream. Ania rushed out the door, weeping at the chaos. "No! No! There's a newborn inside! Stop this!" she screamed.

An inquisitor lunged for her, but Urszula swept her blade upward and severed the attacker's sword arm.

"Get inside," Urszula gritted out. "Close the door, wet a cloth, cover your mouths, and stay low to the ground. Don't come out unless I tell you." As she beat back the leader, Urszula's wild eyes shifted to Brygida.

"And you, do something useful! You lost your blade, but you still have your hands!"

Urszula's words broke whatever indecision had frozen her. Screams and yelling pierced through her skull, and time raced like an arrow.

Ania hadn't moved, shaking and staring at the inquisitors.

Brygida shoved her inside and slammed the door shut.

She ran for the barrel of rainwater by her door as Urszula snarled at an injury. Brygida filled a bucket and threw its water over the flames. Over and over until the barrel was too low to fill again. But the roof's fire continued blazing.

More water. She needed more water.

With the bucket in hand, she ran to the well. The slow crank pulling up the water took forever. Someone shrieked, and the mark on Brygida's hand throbbed.

The demons. They'd been drawn in by the blood and chaos.

"No!" She dragged the bucket over the top of the well and sprinted around to the front of the cottage, where Urszula knelt on one knee, clutching a bleeding shoulder as she swung her red-stained sword fiercely.

From the inky black shadows between the trees, dark figures emerged. Demons. Matoha led them, his sharp, dagger-like teeth glistening with the blood of inquisitors.

The other demons ravaged the black-cloaked crowd, some taking the inquisitors in too-large hands and crunching their bodies in half, others consuming them whole with enormous maws. Teeth broke flesh and claws raked skin as mortal screams burbled to silence. Others faded into the distance as demons chased fleeing inquisitors into the wood.

Bodies of the fallen lay everywhere.

The fire—

The fire. There was no time—

The lives of the mother and child came before anything else. She tossed the bucket, dousing only a little more of what remained of the flames on the house. It would take many more to put them out. Too many. She had to get Jadwiga and her baby out of there, but not while demons roamed free.

The demons... She raised her hand, and with all the power of her mark, she froze them in place.

The demons stopped as one, all turning to her. A hunger lit their gazes. They wanted to tear, to destroy, to kill everyone here, and if she didn't have control of them, she would be included in that number.

Scrambling back from the horde, Urszula panted hard, blood splattered on her face and the bodies of the dead at her feet. Their hungry gazes turned to her and her bleeding shoulder.

They wouldn't make a meal out of her friend. Not while she had something to say about it. As Urszula had said, without her magic she'd lost her blade, but these demons were her hands. Time to use them.

"Help me put out the fire," Brygida commanded.

The demons bowed, and those with hands helped carry water to extinguish the flames or tossed dirt to smother what remained, while Brygida went in to save Jadwiga and her baby from the smoke. The three of them huddled on the floor together, the infant squalling as Jadwiga clutched a wet rag over his mouth and nose. Brygida helped her and Ania up, then brought them outside where all had gone quiet.

They were all dead. All the inquisitors.

She toppled to the ground. So much death. They couldn't all be dead, could they? On her hands and knees, she stumbled amongst the bodies, trying to look for a sign of life among them.

"These things are under your control." Urszula's voice trembled as she'd never before heard.

The demons had put out the flames on the cottage and now waited at attention for her next command.

Yes, it was terrifying. It was shocking. All of it. She nodded her head as she frantically searched across the torn limbs and discarded bloody body parts of the inquisitors. Human lives, gone.

All these women... Had they truly been evil, or only brainwashed by the Dog of Weles, rendered little more than the tools he used to do his dirty work? They hadn't needed to die, but their own choices had damned them, their lives wasted on hatred and manipulation. More bodies added to the death toll the Dog of Weles had amassed.

Killing women went against the core of her beliefs, serving Mokosza, the protector of all women, even the wicked ones who would hurt their own. It was what made the cult so terrifying, their use of women against women. She should have stopped the demons, before it could get this far. How else could she find redemption, if she stood by while more women died?

Would she ever be allowed home?

They would have killed you. You were right to use your power. You are stronger with us. Forget Mokosza, and give in to your true power fully. Their voices whispered over, like serpents slithering across her skin. She shook her head. If she never regained Mokosza's favor, she could never see Mama and Mamusia again, never return to the place of her birth.

The baby cried, and Jadwiga tried to soothe him.

"We should get them out of here. Urszula stood tall and grim faced despite her injuries, although she did clutch at her bleeding shoulder.

Brygida clambered up onto shaky legs. As she passed by one of the fallen, the inquisitor leaped up with a scream, dagger in her hand.

Reaching out desperately, Brygida caught her wrist. The inquisitor threw her back, wrestling her to the ground.

The demons closed in but moved no closer without her command.

"You don't deserve to live," the woman said, baring her teeth. "I'll toss you into the Mouth of Weles, just like we did that old witch." Madness flared in her gaze, crazed and inarguable, as she bore down with the dagger, just above Brygida's throat.

This inquisitor had killed Anita. And now wanted to kill *her*.

It would be easy to beckon the demons, to extinguish this life. No more than a crook of her finger. A thought. The dark rage bubbled up inside of her, the urgent whispers of the demons surrounded her, and she needed only kill this woman, for Anita and all the other witches who'd fallen before her. She had that power, right here within her grasp, the same power that had killed all those who had threatened Mamusia.

Give in. Accept the darkness, the demons hissed. *Take the power.*

Black smoke snaked out of the mark on her palm, consuming her fingers, her hand, her wrist in darkness, until her hand appeared as shadow itself, tipped in demon-like claws.

Her grip tightened. Her strength swelled as she twisted the woman's arm back, eliciting a shout.

The cries stoked a flame in her, a greed, a hunger for vengeance that would only be sated with this woman's blood.

FALL OF THE REAPER

The demons howled, grunted, and cackled as she forced the dagger from the inquisitor's grip. It fell to the ground, beyond her reach. But she didn't need the blade to finish off this zealot.

Someone like this, with such a corrupt worldview she tried to enforce upon all, didn't deserve to live. She didn't deserve to stand on these holy witchlands. She wasn't a woman, wasn't a human, but as much a demon as any among the trees now, but for the human mask she wore.

The inquisitor struggled against her until she used her dead weight to pull Brygida to the ground with her, but Brygida came up on top, pinning her body. With the preternatural strength of Weles coursing through her, further struggle was futile. She could press any point, press and press until the light died from these eyes. It was a much quicker, less terrifying death than Anita and the other witches had suffered, but at least there would be one fewer inquisitor in the world to hurt anyone.

A raven squawked, and Brygida looked up. It sat on her charred roof. Mokosza's messenger.

For a moment, it was as if she floated outside her body. The inquisitor had snot and tears running down her terrified red face, her hair tangled with leaves and grass. A woman. Protected of Mokosza. And Brygida had been prepared to kill her.

This wasn't her. For a moment, the darkness had

nearly consumed her and twisted her thoughts to do something she could have never forgiven herself for.

Finish her. Accept the darkness within. Matoha was right beside her, red eyes gleaming.

No, this wasn't who she was. This wasn't who her mothers had raised her to be. And by indulging this impulse, it would be closing the door on her ever returning home, or regaining Mokosza's favor again. And worse, it would be wrong.

Power was within her grasp, yes, the power to avenge, to harm, to kill. She needed only to reach out and take it. Simply because she could, however, didn't make it just. No, that was the corrupted thought of the Dog of Weles, and those like him, who would grasp and grasp and grasp until the world choked on blood and collapsed in flames. It was simple and crude, while true justice was difficult. She had to be stronger than the corruption and those whose minds it tainted, stronger to deny her anger that reach, that taking.

But she was stronger. And in that moment of temptation, she let that strength fill her up instead of the corruption.

She eased back the pressure on the woman's body, who wheezed, gulping in breaths.

"Bring me something to bind her hands and feet," Brygida hissed to Urszula.

Lying prone, eyes darting about madly, the inquisitor's mask fell away, if only for a moment, and beneath it all was just a scared person wanting to live. And in those mad eyes, a reflection of death stirred, or maybe a reflection of life, depending on the ravens.

Urszula brought rope, and together, they bound the inquisitor's arms behind her back. "What do you want to do... with her?" Urszula asked, her voice measured and hoarse.

The same Urszula who visited her regularly, who didn't flinch at battle, eyed her warily now, and Brygida felt exposed. Try as she might, she couldn't escape the dark power that dwelled within her. And it would continue to separate her from the rest of the world. Each time Urszula looked at her now, would it be with a measure of fear?

Brygida's heart sank, but this was no time to lick her wounds. She'd done everything to unnerve Urszula and deserved the wariness. "We should bring this inquisitor back to the manor for punishment. And Jadwiga needs to be taken from here. This place is no longer safe."

Matoha had slunk back into the woods, and the raven was gone, as if it had never been there at all. But she felt it. They both waited for her, waited to test her conviction further. Perhaps this was part of the challenge that Mokosza had set for her.

With the prisoner captured and subdued for now, it was time to take Jadwiga back home. Her bleeding had subsided, which was a good sign, but her pallor remained. Urszula would have to pull her in the old donkey cart while Brygida would see that their prisoner didn't escape.

Normally, given Jadwiga's condition, she would have had her continue resting, but there was no guarantee that the cult wouldn't return in greater numbers. She had to get them home, and as long as she walked alongside them, Mokosza willing they'd come to no harm, from human hands or demon.

As they passed through the Grobowski manor's gates, the guards rushed forward. Ania and a flock of servants helped Jadwiga from the cart, with the sleeping baby in her arms.

They cooed over the new arrival, and Jadwiga beamed. "We must tell Nikodem and Anatol the good news," she said to a servant as they hurried her toward the manor.

Ania remained by the cart, smiling despite the overbright sheen of her eyes.

"You've saved my daughter," Ania said, taking Brygida's hand. "I can never repay you."

"There is no need for thanks," Brygida replied, gazing at the small, wrinkled face of the newborn before the servants ushered Jadwiga into the manor with her son.

Ania nodded, then headed inside.

With a few words from Urszula, the guards took the inquisitor, who kicked and screamed.

"You cannot contain me," she spat.

You should not have let her live. You could still kill her. From the shadows, Matoha's red eyes gleamed where the others could not see him. Mokosza had no punishment for women who harmed women, but Weles was less merciful.

She'd be lying to say the temptation wasn't great; handing this vile woman over for fair trial felt too kind when considering her victims. But the cycle of blood and fire had to end, the corruption healed.

"That woman and her child are cursed by your touch!" The inquisitor jerked her head toward the manor's entrance.

"Shut your flapping gums, hag!" Urszula roared, and one of the guards shoved the prisoner to her knees.

No, this inquisitor had it wrong. Tonight she had guided a new life into the world. She would never fall into the traps of the cult or give into those dark desires.

"The prophet will see you punished for this. All of you," the woman raved as the guards dragged her away. She spat vitriol the entire time until a door slammed behind her.

Urszula spoke with the guards, gesturing angrily as she gave them orders and information on the Cult of Weles.

"If there's nothing else," Brygida said, "I'll head

back." The cottage would need some tending if she didn't want the rain to pour through her roof.

With a shake of her head, Urszula approached. "Not so fast. Nikodem wants to see you."

About his new baby? Not if Urszula's dour face was any indication. "About what?"

"What else? The cult," Urszula gritted out, before leading the way inside.

Brygida followed her in, a dozen questions on her tongue. Hadn't they just faced the cult? Did Nikodem want to hear what had happened? But if so, he could have asked Urszula, Jadwiga, or Ania. Why did he need *her*?

Urszula guided her upstairs, then dismissed two guards to knock on an oaken door. After a few minutes, a disheveled Anatol came to the door, wearing only a pair of breeches and an open robe, exposing a sleek but strong form. "Good. You're both here."

Clearing her throat, Brygida looked away. "Can this wait until morning?"

"It cannot," Anatol said. "Nikodem wants to speak with you both. The cult is on the move."

He showed them to a sitting area to one end of his room while he tossed clothes aside and picked up a shirt. Anatol disappeared behind a changing screen while Brygida stood by the seats.

"Nikodem will be here shortly. He couldn't wait a moment to see his son." Anatol came back around with a smile on his face. "Ah, and here is the proud father now."

Nikodem strode in, a glow about his usual blank features and a half smile as he shook his head.

"Anatol, you must see him. He's beautiful... my son." His smile widened.

"I was just going there myself." Anatol put a hand on Nikodem's chest. "Congratulations. You will make a wonderful father." They stared into one another's eyes, lost in a happy moment that felt too personal to interrupt.

Urszula tapped her foot and sighed. "We've waited long enough, Nikodem! What's going on? They tried to burn down Brygida's cottage as Jadwiga gave birth to your heir."

Nikodem cleared his throat, and Anatol shook his head as he made his exit. "Thank you, Brygida, for bringing my son into the world safely. As for the Dog of Weles, I learned tonight that he has already conquered most of the surrounding regions, and now his army approaches Rubin. If he sweeps it up, Granat will have enemies on all sides."

His *army*?

Mama. Mamusia... Kaspian. If the Dog of Weles had an army as Nikodem claimed, then they were *all* in danger. "Will your father come to Rubin's aid?"

"He's not here," Urszula answered, kneading her hands into her thighs. "He left just this afternoon for

Jadwiga's region. There's been problems with the cult there as well. But in his absence"—she met her brother's gaze squarely—"Nikodem's order can allow us to mobilize an army," Urszula said through clenched teeth.

"Already done, sister," Nikodem murmured. "Before he left, Tata said he'd gather an allied army. He thought the battlefield would be Granat, but I've sent word about Rubin. It'll take time."

"We need to warn them." Brygida pounded a fist onto her palm. "Otherwise they may not see the attack coming."

"Warn? No, we need to strike." Urszula gestured toward the door. "We need to strike now, while we have them on the back foot." Urszula rose and paced the room, but Nikodem dropped into her vacated space.

"Alone, we don't have the numbers," Nikodem replied, and before Urszula could shoot back, he continued. "The cult's army may not be in Rubin yet, but the cult is present." He stared into the fire, hardly moving while Urszula continued to rage. "The Dog of Weles is methodical in his process... He conquers the minds of the common people before coming for the head of the lord. That is what the lord of Rubin is dealing with right now, and if he loses, Granat may fall, too."

Loses.

It would mean Kaspian losing his *head* to the Dog of Weles.

She swallowed over a lump in her throat, curling her marked palm into a fist. "I won't let them."

"Good. Neither will I," Nikodem said to her, rising as well.

"Nor I." Urszula clasped her fist to her heart.

The Dog of Weles would be in for a shock. The cult would assume she couldn't leave Granat's witchlands, but she had stood up to the Dog of Weles once, and she would do it again.

CHAPTER 7

Like most nights, the Duma Inn hummed with voices. The patrons gathered around in huddled groups, clutching tankards of beer, while laughter carried on the air. But as Kaspian entered, the voices hushed and all eyes turned toward him. These weren't the same sort of hostile gazes he'd experienced the last time he'd made his way here, but it wasn't exactly welcoming either.

If Mama knew he was here, she would surely scold him; lords didn't come amongst their people and mingle like this, or so she said. But despite his and Stefan's best efforts to tease out information about who was spreading the rumors through the village, they'd come up with nothing but dead ends. Rumors lived and breathed where people gathered, and other than the manor house, no place anywhere near here held more people at any given time than this inn.

Stefan swaggered through the tavern, greeting people along the way before claiming a table nearby. To Stefan, this was a familiar place, a home away from home, where he shared stories, laughs, and beers with friends and acquaintances. For Stefan, there was warmth here, comfort, ease.

Shifting from foot to foot, Kaspian glanced about the place. Behind the bar, Agata stood with her arms crossed over her chest, beady eyes trained on him. Although there was no cleaver in her hand, he could still envision it glinting in the sun, about to separate him from his manhood. He shuddered.

Best to keep his attention on the task at hand. He sat down next to Stefan. "Are you sure these people will talk to us?" he whispered to Stefan, who waved over the barmaid with an easy smile.

Stefan put in his order, and as she sauntered away, he gave Kaspian an incredulous once-over. "To you? Not a chance. You're their lord. You think we can walk up to any old person and just say: why, my good sir, are you plotting an uprising in the village?"

Kaspian sighed. "I'm not that naive. But why bring me here if they won't talk to me?"

"Because I need a distraction."

Perun's bright lightning. "A distraction?" Kaspian quirked an eyebrow. Somehow he had a bad feeling about this. Stefan's distractions usually left him making apologies.

Stefan shrugged a shoulder. "Like I said, they're not going to just spill their guts to me, even if I ask questions. Everyone knows where my loyalties lie."

And yet, with every one of Stefan's words, he could feel his coin pouch weigh less and less. He leaned away, eyeing the door. "I don't know if I like where this is going..."

Stefan tilted his head slightly to the right. "See that group over there?"

Kaspian started to turn his head to look—

"Don't look at them," Stefan said in a harsh whisper.

Kaspian grunted. He couldn't wait to hear how he was supposed to see a group of people without looking.

The barmaid came around at that moment and delivered two tankards of beer. Kaspian wouldn't touch his, but it would look even more suspicious if he sat here without one. Still, the golden amber contents were a temptation, especially when he could use some liquid courage.

Stefan winked at her. "I have one more request of you, if you don't mind?"

She fluttered her eyelashes. "What's that?"

"Could you get a round of drinks on behalf of his lordship for that table over there in the corner?"

"I—" Kaspian started to protest, but Stefan's heel dug into his beneath the table.

The barmaid frowned, but as Stefan made eyes at her, she nodded and brought the drinks to the table. There had always been little in this village Stefan couldn't get with a wink and a smile from a young woman. Older ones, too.

Kaspian was neither. And although he normally wouldn't have missed the coin, during a blight, every *denar* mattered. "Why are you spending my coin?"

"You buy them drinks, and they'll be obliged to thank you, and while their attention is on you, I can slip this into their drinks." He held up a sachet of powder.

"Do I even want to know what that is?" Kaspian sighed and massaged his temples.

Stefan put the sachet back in his breast pocket. "Just a little something a friend of mine gave me that can help loosen tongues." Stefan drank deeply of his beer.

"A friend?" Kaspian leaned in a bit closer. Perhaps Stefan was ready to loosen his own tongue. "Is this friend the one you've been disappearing to visit lately?"

Mid-gulp, Stefan spit his beer back into his cup. "I don't know what you're talking about," he said nonchalantly into his cup.

"Mm," Kaspian teased. Either the manor had the worst fences in the region, forcing Stefan to constantly chase down horses, or Stefan had a special... friend. A secret friend.

He'd seen Stefan heading over toward Nina's farm

on many occasions. "You don't have to hide it from me, just because—"

Just because Brygida's gone. He couldn't even finish the sentence. Most of the time he just tried not to think about her, pretended to himself that he was interested in searching out a bride. It was better this way, he tried telling himself. No matter what he felt, it was impractical. They were too different after all, weren't they?

But when he thought about Stefan marrying and moving on, maybe even joining Nina on the Baran farm, his own future felt desperately lonely. Solitude had been liberating once, a little space to think, to daydream, to paint. But after meeting the other half of his soul, and being parted from her, solitude had become a prison, its confinement filled only with the painful longing to complete his soul once more. He'd had enough of solitude, yes. And long ago.

"She's going to come back," Stefan said somberly.

No, Brygida had gone for good, it seemed. It had been months, with no word from her, no visit, nothing.

Mama had said she'd find him a bride, and once she'd choose for him, maybe he wouldn't argue this time. Maybe a wife would ease the pain...

The group of farm hands sitting by the fire got their drinks and, upon hearing who had sent them, rose from their table and came to surround him and Stefan. They were familiar faces, from the Malicki manor.

"My lord, we appreciate your generosity," one man said thoughtfully, eyeing the table.

"Please join us." Stefan gestured to the empty seats around them.

The men shared a look before taking seats next to them. Once everyone was seated, they all looked at one another in silence. They appeared as though they'd come to relax after work, still in their mud-encrusted boots and roughspun shirts and breeches, some dusty and sweat stained. Bits of hay dotted one man's hair, and black dirt packed beneath most of their fingernails. A group of farmhands, and likely ones who'd known and been friends with Julian. This certainly could not go wrong at all. In any way whatsoever.

What to even say? Doubtful these men wanted to be asked about their work by a lord. Or talked down to if he tried to bridge their differences. Better something innocuous, something simple. He cleared his throat. "I came here to make sure the people of our village are happy."

No one could find fault with that, could they?

Stefan raised a palm to his forehead, and the men all shared questioning looks. As the silence stretched, it became so quiet Kaspian could count the beats of his own heart. Surely one of these men would have mercy and say something. He bounced a nervous foot beneath the table. Still nothing. Where was the distraction part of Stefan's plan?

"We are, my lord," one of the men said at last, raising his tankard of beer.

Oh, praise Perun. A merciful man.

"Good. Good." Kaspian tapped his hands on the table.

One man drained his tankard and set it back down. "Thank you for your hospitality, my lord, but I think we should be heading home now."

No, not yet. Stefan hadn't even put in the powder yet.

"Wait." Kaspian stood, and the entire tavern turned to look at him, including Agata, who frowned in his direction. He cleared his throat. "Agata, another round for everyone on me."

The entire tavern erupted into cheers. Stefan stared up at him, mouth agape as Kaspian shrugged his shoulders. What else could he do? He clearly had no charm but a sizable sum of *denary*.

"You'd better have the coin on you to cover that boast in full," Agata called to him, glowering. "I'm not walking all the way to the manor to get paid."

The pouch at his hip should cover it, but...

Agata.

Agata was the center of the village. She wielded a lot of influence amongst the peasants. It was she who had incited the mob against him after the Feast of the Mother...

He'd assumed she couldn't be behind the saboteurs,

and while he wasn't convinced she was the mastermind, it didn't mean she wasn't a part of the greater plot. Perhaps *she* was the one who had helped spread the rumors.

Kaspian took out his coin pouch and walked it over to the bar, then set it down for Agata. "I hope this is enough?"

She picked it up, weighing it in her hand, and then tucked it into her apron. It looked like he wasn't even going to get the pouch back. He sighed. It wasn't worth the threat of the cleaver to ask for it.

To the barmaid, she said, "Bring everyone drinks."

The barmaid did as she was told, and as drinks were passed around, the people cheered, drinking deeply. Conversation returned to its normal flow, and he sat back down at the table.

"I hope you'll stay for another round?" he asked the men.

They nodded somewhat reluctantly, and when the tankards arrived, Stefan handed them out one by one, and with a flick of his wrist, he dropped the powder into their drinks.

"Cheers?" Kaspian brought the ale to his lips but did not drink, although the temptation was maddening.

As they chugged their beer, with every drink, their postures slumped and their eyes began to glaze over. It had to be working.

"I've been wondering..." Stefan swirled his own

untainted beer. "There seems to be an awful lot of rumors going around about our Lord Rubin."

One of the men slammed his hand on the table. "The bastard. Living in that manor without a care for us hardworking men."

Tell me how you really feel. Ducking lower in his chair, Kaspian rubbed his chin but remained silent. But this was what he'd wanted, wasn't it? To better understand the hardships of his people, so he could be a more effective ruler. He could hardly achieve that while feeling sorry for himself.

"I've been wondering: would it be easier if he was gone?" Stefan asked brightly.

Thanks, Stef.

The men all grumbled, but no one spoke up.

"What was that?" Stefan leaned forward.

"I don't know if he would be any better than the next rich lord," one of the men said with a shrug. "They're all the same, aren't they?"

Kaspian frowned. Was the potion not working?

"Have you heard of anyone who wants to cause trouble in the village, wants things to change, perhaps?" Stefan prompted.

The man squinted. "There's those troublemakers from today." He shook his head. "Disrespectful, stealing from the mouths of the innocent." He hiccuped and swayed. This was going nowhere and fast.

Behind the bar, Agata continued to watch him,

eyes narrowed. Stefan could try his luck here, but he had sight of better game. He got up and walked over to the bar. "Mind if I ask you some questions?"

"I do, but it's not as though I can refuse the lord of Rubin." With a raise of her eyebrows, she leaned forward on the bar, if she were trying to intimidate him. It wouldn't work this time.

He leaned in, too, meeting her in the middle. "I'll be blunt: I know it's you who's spreading rumors that I killed Roksana."

She jerked her head backward. "Is that so?"

With a scoff, Kaspian shook his head. She'd brought an entire mob to punish him for that crime. She couldn't now pretend that had never happened. "That day, you were going to...." he trailed off with a vague wave downward.

"Ah. Yes." A fleeting predatory grin. "And I paid for my part in that."

Tata had put her in the stocks for three days. It had been a deserved punishment, but he could see her being bitter about it still.

He ground his teeth. "You still think I'm guilty. You want to see a new lord in my place."

She blew out a breath and drummed her fingers on the bar. "I'll be the first to admit I am not happy with your family, and I still say your rotten brother deserves to pay for what he did. And if he ever comes here, I'll do to him what I nearly did to you." She pointed at him with her cleaver.

Agata hated his family. And after what his brother had done to her daughter, she had every reason to. But these rumors wouldn't punish Henryk; they'd only hurt the village, and perhaps the region. "Then you admit to sowing discord among the people?"

She shook her head. "I never said that. All I said was that I don't like your family. I know you didn't kill Roksana, because if you had, then the witches would have seen justice done. I saw the power of that young Reaper that day, and there isn't a doubt in my mind that she's not blessed with Mokosza's power."

She seemed sincere in her conviction. It didn't make sense. "Then if it wasn't you who spread the rumors, who was it?"

She shrugged. "That's none of my concern, now is it?"

"The village's welfare isn't your concern?" He jerked his head toward the tavern full of people. "If the rumors harm your clientele, who's going to come here to line your pockets?"

With a half-laugh, she returned to her work. "I already got all your coin, my lord. You can do your own duties."

There was no more use questioning her.

"And tell your stable hand to keep his eyes—and his everything—off Justyna," Agata said with a huff. "She's my least clumsy barmaid so far, and I won't have her become a behind-the-barn kind of girl."

"I'm sure he'd let her inside the barn," Kaspian mumbled under his breath, and Agata threw a dishrag at him. He caught it with a sour smile and rejoined Stefan at their table, where the farm hands had passed out, their tankards turned over. "Any luck?"

Stefan raised his hands from the table, uncovering an assortment of coins and a button. "I won a hand of cards."

His stomach sinking, Kaspian nodded toward the door, and they headed back home. Neither of them said a word as they walked.

Czarnobrzeg was becoming a place he no longer recognized. Behind every tree or any building they passed, there could be spies, thieves, saboteurs, or worse. Someone plotted against him, of that he was certain. The question remained: who? Perhaps Stefan had heard something useful.

They reconvened in the barn, where Demon and the other horses were eating their evening meal. After checking all the stalls to make sure that they were alone, Stefan waved him in front of Demon's stall. "Any luck with Agata?"

Kaspian shook his head. "No, but I don't think she's behind it."

"The farm hands were a bust, too. They didn't know

anything about the Cult of Weles, or why those two stole the grain and seed."

Kaspian sighed and ran his hand through his hair. "There has to be a leader, someone who has something to gain." If it wasn't Agata, and Dariusz was dead, then who could it be?

Stefan's gaze flickered to the door.

"It's the Dog of Weles," Stryjek said from the barn's doorway. He strolled inside in his woolen robe and slippers.

"Who or what is the Dog of Weles?" Kaspian asked. Demon poked his head out of his stall and lunged for Kaspian's elbow, but Stefan shoved his nose back inside, grumbling under his breath at the gelding.

"The Dog of Weles is the cult's leader," Stryjek said, eyeing Demon and leaning against a stall just out of reach. "He's been causing all sorts of trouble across the regions. I came here because I figured he wouldn't bother with such a tiny backwater, but it seems like he's set his eyes on Rubin at last. They've been recruiting locals for months. Haven't you figured it out?"

"Yes, that's exactly why we're spending all this time trying to figure it out," Stefan remarked. "Because we've definitely figured it out."

"Quiet, stable boy," Stryjek scolded half-heartedly, but Stefan slumped a little. At least he made a show of appearing chastised.

Kaspian shook his head. "Why didn't you tell me this sooner?"

Stryjek shrugged. "I tried to. Remember those rabble-rousers Agata tossed out of the tavern? Those were Cult of Weles members."

If the cult was behind this and was as powerful as Stryjek claimed, then this was much more serious than they'd realized. Far past sussing out rumors and putting thieves in the stocks.

He would need to reach out to allies as swiftly as possible. It was time he asked Granat for help.

CHAPTER 8

Brygida could feel it before she saw it, soothing like a gentle embrace. It was the familiar sweet scent of spring, the calls of redpolls and siskins, and the shallow-hilled landscape that rolled into home. As they approached the village, her heart swelled upon seeing it. She was home at last.

The Mrok woods were bursting with green life; the dandelion roots and nettle leaf that she would harvest with Mamusia at this time of year would be in bloom. When she'd been a girl, they had braided crowns of globe-flowers to wear in their hair, and even Mama would laugh and play with them. On warm spring days, she would dip into the Skawa River and or its stream that fed into Mroczne Lake and let the cold water rush over her.

What she would give to run to the forest, to the

cottage, to fall into Mama and Mamusia's embraces. To touch their faces, to hear Mamusia's laugh, and even Mama's scolding would be welcome in this moment.

She held up her Weles-marked hand. The crescent had not faded. She'd tried not to use the dark power, resisted its allure. She lived by Mokosza's way, and even after sparing the inquisitor, saving Jadwiga in childbirth, cleansing Anita's forest—none of it had made a difference. She was still fallen. Mokosza's challenge was a difficult one, and no clear path presented itself.

As much as she longed for home, she could not return to the cottage, not yet. When she had broken Mokosza's sacred laws, she'd been banished from her witchlands and could not set foot on them until this mark disappeared. Not until she had repented fully.

Nikodem, on horseback beside her, waited without a word. She was thankful for his silence. Because if he asked her if she was all right, or otherwise tried to comfort her, she might just crumple into a sobbing heap at his feet. She needed to be strong, for Mamusia, Mama, and Kaspian.

As a hazel grouse scurried across their path, she tore her gaze away from the forest and back to the land ahead, past scorched farmlands.

Why they'd been burned, she couldn't be sure, but was she too late? Had the cult already attacked? "Nikodem..."

"I know," he said grimly. "It could be blight."

And he seemed to have the truth of it; apart from a few burned fields, the old familiar landscape was just the same. And there, in the distance, was the manor, Kaspian's home.

Despite every reason to the contrary, her stomach fluttered. After months apart, even if he wasn't happy to see her, she wanted to see his face. She wanted to take him in with her own eyes, make sure he was all right. The way they had parted had hung around her neck like a stone, and if they could at least be friends, that burden would lessen.

As they rode through the village, farmers working their land, plowing fields, or tending to their livestock stopped to watch them pass, shading their eyes and squinting in her direction. Nikodem had suggested she keep her scythe wrapped and hidden away, but after the banquet at Anatol's family manor, he had styled her as his advisor—complete with lavish robes, a badge with the Granat symbol of the bear, and a coiffure befitting a person of her new position, as Anatol had explained. Jadwiga had taught her how to braid away from her face and plait voluminously in the back. It would all grant her status, they'd said, and avoid how some had tried to dismiss her.

Fancy red robes, a badge, and a new hairstyle wouldn't change her in the eyes of the Czarnobrzeg villagers, but if she seemed to be in Nikodem's service, perhaps at least Lady Rubin wouldn't despise her so openly.

Although there was no telling how Kaspian would react. His father had died, and she'd had to leave when he'd most needed support. After that, she didn't expect a warm welcome.

And any one of these people could be cultists in disguise, prepared to attack. It had been these people who'd turned against Mamusia, who even now fell to the whispers of the cult.

You could defeat them all. You have that power. You need not fear them, Matoha whispered in her mind. Over days of travel, he had followed her, staying out of sight, but always there, whispering in her ear. And it wasn't just him; other demons had followed her from Anita's forest. Even if they didn't speak to her, she saw traces of them, destroyed deer carcasses, footprints outside her tent when she woke in the morning. There was no escaping them, just as there seemed to be no way to heal the mark.

Brygida ignored Matoha as the gates of Wolski manor opened for them. The servants working in the yard looked up, chatting excitedly, some of them rushing into the manor.

Nikodem swung down from the saddle, then helped her dismount.

"Brygida," an excited voice called, and Stefan

rushed over to her, a smile splitting his features. He rubbed his hands into his shirt. "Is it really you?"

"It is." She embraced him, inhaling the comforting scent of horse and fresh hay. The courtyard's many gazes fixed on her, wide eyed as if she were a dog walking on its hind legs.

Taking a step back, Stefan looked her up and down with a whistle. "Life's been treating you well, I see." His eyes flickered toward Nikodem, who instructed his men, and then back to her. "What have you been doing for the past six months?"

"Taming demons, mostly."

Stefan's mouth dropped open and shook his head. "You must be joking."

She most certainly was not. "It is the truth."

A half-smile briefly claimed his lips. "I shouldn't expect any less from you."

"How about you?" She looked past his shoulder at the paddock, but Demon wasn't outside. "Still chasing horses around all of Rubin?"

Stefan opened his mouth, but before he could answer, Nikodem stepped between them, interrupting their reunion.

"We need to speak with Lord Rubin, as soon as possible."

"Brygida?"

That voice, *his* voice, stroked down her back like a feather.

She glanced over her shoulder, over the expanse of red cloaking it, to where Kaspian stood at the top of the steps leading into the manor house, crowding the doorway.

At one time, she would have just called this face of his expressionless, but she'd learned better; he was at a loss, multiple expressions competing at once, and so he allowed none.

His straw-blond hair looked lighter somehow, as if he'd spent more time in the sun, or perhaps the sunshine now illumed it a little more than she remembered. Against the deep navy of his open jacket, it was all the lighter.

His arms hung at his sides, but his fingers—one or two twitched slightly, the way they always had before he'd touched her. Their affectionate request mirrored what stirred in that sparkling cornflower-blue gaze, a question, a thousand, and a glimpse of an answer.

Behind him, his mother swatted at his shoulder. "Kaspian, you're blocking the doorway. Kaspian—"

His lips parted, and even as he stood aside for Lady Rubin to pass and stride down the stairs, he didn't look away.

A touch ghosted across her mouth, the brush of his kiss when he'd been blindfolded in Granat. She breathed in deeply and inhaled memory, the scent of paints on his fingers, the stroke of them on her cheek.

It was all she could do to swallow.

Lady Rubin strode into her line of sight with an unexpected smile on her face. Kaspian approached behind her.

From his golden hair down to the tips of his polished boots, he was exactly as she remembered.

"What are you doing here?" He extended his hand slightly, as if to reach for her. She was tempted to take it, to grab on and never let go again.

"I asked Brygida to join me on this trip," Nikodem answered for her bewildered mouth.

Kaspian's gaze shifted to Nikodem, and then to Brygida, and it was as if a different face slid over his as he crossed his arms. Whatever enchantment had fluttered between them had broken, replaced by a lined brow and narrowed eyes. "Have you been in Granat all this time?"

Why was his tone so cold? That was all he had to say after not seeing each other for months? Perhaps this was who they were now, after she had left without providing comfort in his hour of need.

She raised her chin. "Yes, I have."

He gave a brisk nod and then turned to Nikodem. "I'm glad you're here, Nikodem. We were about to send a messenger to ask for your family's aid. The Cult of Weles has infiltrated Rubin."

"That is why we have come," Nikodem replied.

"Your timing couldn't be better, then. Please, come

inside. Both of you must be tired from your journey."
He gestured them toward the house.

Lady Rubin joined Brygida, walking alongside her.
"Come with me, Brygida. I'll have a bath drawn for
you." There was nothing but sweetness and care in
Lady Rubin's invitation. Was this some daydream?

Lady Rubin had been nothing but cold to her the
last time they'd seen each other, but now she was as
content as a fox with a hazel grouse chick beneath its
paw. Once upon a time, Lady Rubin had wanted her
gone, and now, it seemed, she'd gotten what she'd
wanted. Perhaps that was it.

But Kaspian... No, she hadn't expected a warm
welcome, but in that fleeting moment when they'd
looked upon each other for the first time in six months,
something had rekindled. Some remnant of warmth
had stirred to life. But just as quickly, he'd suffocated it.

What did she know of love? She'd never been with a
man, and had only ever felt deeply for one. Had it been
love? Or had she been foolish, as Halina had told her?
Halina had said men like him only wanted one thing,
that they didn't truly care.

And when her mothers had needed his help, he had
turned his back on her. When it had mattered most,
he'd abandoned her.

"Are you all right, my dear?" Lady Rubin guided her
inside.

"Yes," she replied quickly. "And a bath would be

most welcome." It was time to wash away thoughts of Kaspian. She had come here for one reason, and that was to save her mothers and the village.

He had abandoned her once, but she wouldn't abandon Czarnobrzeg, its people, and those she cared about most to the Cult of Weles.

CHAPTER 9

Kaspian could hardly sleep. How could he, when Brygida was under this same roof? For months, he'd pushed away thoughts of her, but now her face and the sound of her voice consumed his thoughts. All this time, she'd been in Granat... and with Nikodem? Had she moved on so quickly? Had he been the only one who'd felt their love had been real?

There had hardly been time to talk last night; Mama had insisted they not press their guests so soon after travel, and Nikodem wasn't exactly the most talkative sort. But the sooner he and Nikodem sorted out the cult, the sooner Nikodem and Brygida could leave together, and he could live his life in peace.

The sun started to rise, and soon the footsteps began, the household doing their morning duties. He had his own, and worrying about a love from his past wasn't important right now. All that mattered was getting this Cult of Weles under control.

He rose and prepared for the day. He buttoned his shirt and stared at himself in the mirror. That was what he wanted, right? He and Brygida were too different. Where had she been in those cold winter days, as he'd grieved for Tata? Where had she been when he'd needed her? In Nikodem's arms.

He clenched his hand into a fist. The less he thought about her and Nikodem together, the better. It would only lead to anger.

He hurried down the stairs and into the main hall, where servants and guards milled about, breaking their fast. And at the far end, Brygida and Nikodem sat, their heads tilted together as they spoke.

Stefan patted him on the shoulder. "They look rather cozy, don't you think?"

Kaspian knocked his hand aside. "I'm happy for her," he forced out in a monotone.

Stefan raised an eyebrow. "Are you sure about that? It looks like you're grinding your teeth."

He tried to unclench his jaw. It didn't matter if Brygida had found someone else. It didn't matter. He repeated over and over in his head as he approached them.

"I won't kill innocents, Nikodem," Brygida said passionately. "These people who are a part of his so-called army, I know they can't all be bad. The lies the

Dog of Weles has been spreading are like an infection of the mind, and they're sick with it. There has to be another way."

"Will you spare these 'sick' zealots when they kill innocent people?" Nikodem shot back.

Brygida sighed and lifted her head. For a moment, their gazes met, and just as it had the first time he'd met her, he felt that strike of Perun's lightning down his spine.

As quickly as their gazes met, she looked away. Damn his heart for betraying him, but he missed her. Despite everything, how she'd hurt him and how she clearly didn't need him anymore, he missed her. It felt as if it had only been days ago when they'd spent those dreamy hours in the forest together.

But this was no time for daydreaming. Those memories would have to stay where they belonged: in the past. Shoving down the feelings, he kept his expression neutral. "I apologize for interrupting you both, but I couldn't help overhearing you say something about an army."

"That's what we came to speak with you about," Nikodem replied. "The Cult of Weles has gathered an army, and they are headed for Rubin."

Headed for...

Panic seized his chest. An army? He'd have to raise troops across all of Rubin, but could he manage it in time? And how would he defeat an army? He'd learned military strategy and knew how to use a sword, but that was no substitute for experienced leadership. Already, a list of a hundred tasks tumbled through his head.

"Thank you for the warning. It sounds as if your father has plans of his own," Kaspian said to Nikodem.

"We are gathering recruits from our loyal vassals, and I advise you to do the same," Nikodem said quietly. "It will take some time before my father can march on the cult here in Rubin, but until then, Brygida and I are at your disposal."

He couldn't look at Brygida, let alone have her at his disposal for any length of time. Besides, what could the two of them do to thwart the cult that he couldn't? Perhaps that was the best course—to learn how to combat the cult's insidious tactics and await Lord Granat's arrival with his forces.

"Let's discuss this further in private." He trusted his household, but someone had to have been working with the cult to allow access to the granary. No one could be trusted.

As he turned to escort them to the study for a private conversation, Rafał approached, with six men-at-arms at his back. Seeing the grim looks on their faces made his stomach drop.

"My lord, an army has made camp on the border. What are your orders?"

"The Cult of Weles. They've come," Brygida said as

she clutched the vial of lake water around her neck. On her palm was a crescent-shaped black mark.

He tore his gaze away from her. Now wasn't the time.

"What shall we do, my lord?" Although Rafał's usual grim expression was firmly in place, a stark pallor accompanied it.

They were unprepared for a confrontation, and if the numbers of the army were as great as Nikodem suspected, they would be destroyed in an instant. But by the same token, he couldn't stand by and let this army walk right into the village. "We go to greet them."

"I'm coming with you." Brygida stood, and her hand brushed against his. On reflex, he pulled away. She jerked her head back and stared at him.

"Your aid would be welcome," he said to them both, trying to keep his voice measured despite his heart hammering in his chest.

"Gather as many men as you are able," Kaspian ordered Rafał, and he strode out before he'd say something he'd regret in front of Brygida.

He was unseasoned when it came to leading an army, but he'd fought demons and survived by thinking on his feet. He could do it again. Arriving with even a small contingent of men would give the appearance that the use of force wasn't off the table. He could bluff, at least enough to keep unconditional surrender out of the conversation. And he could stall if necessary, ideally long enough for Lord Granat to arrive with his forces. He'd leave Mama here, in case the worst happened and Rubin did need to negotiate terms for its people.

But... with Brygida here, it wouldn't come to any of that. She was powerful enough to dispel a mob, and could drain a man of his blood. What were these cultists against her? If she was with them, they'd make it out alive, and if the cultists tried anything, he'd seen what her wrath of the blood could do.

Once everything was prepared, they all mounted up and rode out. Her hood pulled far over her head, Brygida followed behind him, and he had to resist the urge to look back at her. All their hope lay with her, with her power, and as much as her return had unsettled him, he was thankful for it.

Tendrils of smoke rose up on the horizon over the treetops. And then, in a clearing, hundreds of tents stretched as far as he could see, more than he'd expected. Even knowing the numbers beforehand, seeing them in the flesh was staggering.

As they approached, women in black armor with white horned serpents emblazoned on their chests greeted them, holding crude spears.

"Who are you, and what are you doing here?" the first woman challenged.

"I'm the lord of Rubin. We've come to speak to your leader."

The women shared looks. "Wait here, and we'll bring the prophet to you."

Prophet? Their leader purported to know the will of Weles? Kaspian nodded, and the second woman walked into the camp, wending her way through the rows of tents.

A crowd came through the tents of people, two lines of women all dressed in the same black armor emblazoned with the white horned serpent. At the rear, a hooded figure followed, his head down.

As the so-called prophet approached, the crowd filed to one side, flanking the man at the center.

"All hail the Prophet of Weles," one of the women called out.

The assembled cultists bowed as one, and then the man in the center pushed back his hood, revealing long golden-blond hair.

It couldn't be. This had to be a nightmare.

"Hello, brother." Henryk looked up with a smile.

CHAPTER 10

Brygida could not have heard him right. Had the Dog of Weles called Kaspian his brother?

The Dog grinned from ear to ear while Kaspian stood with his mouth hanging open. "Are you not going to greet me, Kaspian? Or have you forgotten my face since I've been gone?"

Kaspian sputtered, and Brygida pushed her mount forward. Brother or not, she would not see him step onto these lands or threaten their people.

Tear out his throat. You know you want to, Matoha whispered in her ear.

She ignored him. But the Dog of Weles slid his gaze to her and his eyes widened. "You." He said it like a caress as his lips curled upward. "You are far from your witchlands."

"Those who are truly chosen by Weles need not be bound to any land," Brygida countered.

The inquisitors who flanked him grasped their weapons, their gazes hungry, like hunting dogs pulling at their leads. If she was going to chase him away, it would mean drawing from her mark. Just as the Dog of Weles had his hounds, she had her own. Their hungry hissing voices filled her ears. Just like Matoha, other demons she'd tamed had followed her. They waited in the woods, prepared to strike at the slightest flick of her wrist.

"Henryk, do you know one another?" Kaspian looked between Brygida and the Dog of Weles.

Henryk?

Henryk, as in the brother who'd raped Agata's daughter, Dorota? Who had been sent away to the priesthood by his parents? *That* Henryk?

He didn't remove his unnerving gaze from her. "We have met once before, little brother. What a coincidence I would meet her again here, at my home."

Did Henryk believe he had the advantage here, because Kaspian was his brother? The Kaspian she knew would never welcome this monster here, let alone help him.

"You were a priest of Perun," Kaspian said, although it sounded more like a question. His eyebrows creased together.

Priest of Perun? What did any of that matter?

He should tell Henryk to leave and never return. Why was he wasting time? Had he already forgotten what the cult had done, what his brother had done?

"That's a long story," Henryk crooned. "One I would like to tell you, Mama, and Tata together."

Kaspian's face drained of color. "Tata passed, just this last winter."

Henryk put a hand to his mouth as if in shock, yet his eyes held no sorrow.

Liar. This Dog knew his father had died; she could see it in his face. He'd smelled blood, and like a fox, he'd come to pick at the bones.

"It must be Weles's will that I come here now, when you need me most of all." Henryk stepped forward, with an easy but confident stride. "I must see our mother."

Kaspian looked around, meeting her gaze for a split-second. She barely restrained a scowl. He couldn't be considering Henryk's words, could he? It was obvious Henryk was trying to manipulate him, to twist him to his will, the way he'd done to all the lost people gathered here.

Kaspian rubbed the back of his neck. "We cannot accommodate you all at the manor."

"I will bring only my most devoted disciples. I know there will be room enough for them." He smiled, all pretenses of grief gone from his radiant face.

Kaspian shifted uncomfortably in his saddle. He would break bread with this rapist, this murderer?

"Are you certain—?" she whispered, but Nikodem rested a gentle hand on her shoulder. He shook his head slowly.

She exhaled through her nose. She'd come here to chase away the Cult of Weles, not see them invited in for dinner.

Perhaps Kaspian was blind to the Dog's manipulations, but she could save them. When she had summoned the mark that day to protect Mamusia at the Mouth of Weles, it had taken nothing at all to kill an entire bloodthirsty mob.

Henryk smiled brightly at his brother, his relaxed bearing so serene, as if he were about to enjoy a sunrise. She'd rather give him a sunset. A final one.

It's not too late, Matoha whispered. *Use your power. Destroy them all. You have the strength to end this here.*

The mark on her palm throbbed. She clutched her hand tighter.

All she had to do was give in to the power within her. Kaspian would be saved, and she would protect the village, avenge all the witches who had fallen to these zealots. This could all end here.

Smoke rose from her mark, and a nearby inquisitor pointed and whispered into her hands.

The Dog smirked, although his gaze darted to her hand and just as quickly returned to serenity. Or a pretense of it. "Will you be joining us, Brygida?"

He knew her name?

What else did he know? Who her mothers were? Where they lived?

Her heartbeat thrummed.

Just take the power, Matoha encouraged. *Destroy him. Now.*

"Brygida?" Kaspian asked, and his concerned face filled her vision.

No. She couldn't do this, not after everything she had done, everything she'd given up to get this far. She wouldn't play right into the Dog's hand.

He wanted to make an example of her, expose her to an army of strangers, ones she wouldn't have had the benefit of having treated, or their lord's favor. But she wouldn't become the effigy he wished to burn.

She would defeat him, but it would be on her own terms, the right way, and without breaking her vow to Mokosza.

The Dog gathered up *his most devoted disciples*, as he called them, and they all made their way back toward the manor.

"I will not." Although she couldn't kill him now as some part of her wished to, she refused to stay under the same roof as this monster. She wouldn't share a meal with him, wouldn't pretend to be civil. She'd rather starve.

"Pity," Henryk replied with mock disappointment as he and his entourage rode past her toward the manor.

Something like a snarl rumbled within her, and she

snapped a glare at him over her shoulder, but Nikodem's hold on her shoulder firmed. Yes, he was right. She took several slow, deep breaths as their group turned to head back as well.

Everyone else could be content to follow this cur's stinking wake and play his games, but she was not. Despite his veneer of gentility, he had teeth, sharp ones, and if he knew her name, her mothers might not be safe.

At the first opportunity, she slipped away and instead headed toward the Perun-struck oak, the border between her witchlands and the outside world.

⚜

KASPIAN COULDN'T SHAKE THE SENSATION OF DREAD creeping over his skin.

Henryk stood in the center of the solarium, the mud crusting his boots flaking off onto Mama's treasured rug. His dark cloak and the women he'd brought with him seemed to cast shadows even in this normally bright and airy place, as if he'd stolen all its light. Perhaps he had.

"Ah, it feels good to be back home." With a casual gesture from Henryk, the woman at his right stepped forward, head bowed, and slid the cloak from his shoulders; bowing on her way out, she exited the room.

Something about the display made his skin crawl—

that dread lingering, maybe, and he had a feeling it would only worsen.

Underneath, Henryk wore a finely tailored shirt and trousers also in the deepest black, with luxurious silken accents. Odd. Henryk had always liked the finer things in life, but priests lived humble lives. When their parents had sent Henryk away, they could have sent him anywhere, but they'd chosen the priesthood of Perun, where he would've been meant to reflect on what he'd done, make amends, and live modestly. It wouldn't have undone the evil he'd wrought upon Dorota, nor had it been true justice, but his parents had seemed to have put some thought into it.

And yet, Henryk had made his way to the head of the Cult of Weles, with no reflection, amends, nor modesty. He'd shirked every consequence of what he'd done, as he always had.

There was a clatter.

Mama stood in the doorway, her face blanched of color, and pewter cups strewn about the floor. Next to her, Iskra whined, nosing Mama's hand.

"Henryk?" Her brow lined, she grasped the door frame with a shaking hand. "What are you doing here?"

Henryk strode toward Mama and took her into a stiff-armed hug. "I've come home! Aren't you happy to see me?" Despite the words, there was something false about them, something theatrical.

Mama looked from left to right as she pulled away,

her lips drawn tight. "Of course... Of course I am." Her gaze continued to dart around the room, resting on Kaspian for the briefest moment of sheer terror.

Henryk smiled and sauntered over to a nearby chair, where he sat and leaned back, one leg slung over the arm. Without a word, one of the women who'd been hovering at his shoulder picked up the pewter cups from the floor and righted them, setting them on a nearby table. Another of his so-called disciples disappeared down the hallway.

"Take a seat." Henryk gestured him and Mama to the other chairs in the solarium.

Kaspian's hands throbbed at his sides. Too much blood filled them, coursed too fast, too hot. A part of him wanted to seize Henryk by the collar and force him to pay for the crimes he had escaped, for Dorota, and for everyone the cult had ever harmed.

Another part of him longed to kill his own brother. Right here. Just for causing that look of sheer terror on their mother's face. Even for a second.

Henryk's "disciple" returned with a bottle of wine, one that had surely come from their own cellar, and poured a glass for him before stepping back again. Would that she were the only one held so completely in Henryk's thrall. But she was one of many.

As much as he'd like to throttle Henryk for daring to come here, an army secured Henryk's life at their border, and until Lord Granat's reinforcements arrived, he'd have to play this game.

Reluctantly, Kaspian took a seat across from Henryk, while Mama continued to stand, her hands grasping the chair in front of her. She had not taken her gaze off Henryk.

"I'm disappointed in you, Mama. You did not write to me about father's passing. Or at all," Henryk said, swirling the wine in his glass. "As his one-time heir, I would have liked to say goodbye." Henryk gave her a lingering look, one many a cat had given its prey.

Mama clutched the chair tighter. "We were told those who serve in the temple of Perun must shed all worldly ties."

Henryk took a long swig of his wine before holding out his glass, and his "disciple" refilled it for him. "Yes, the temple does like to demand such things of its acolytes, doesn't it?"

Mama shifted from foot to foot, still clutching the back of her chair. Iskra growled, but Mama glanced at her dog and nodded toward the door. "Iskra, out."

With a distressed whine, Iskra looked toward the doorway and at Henryk before heading out. Had Mama worried Henryk would hurt her dog?

Henryk smiled charismatically. It was a familiar expression, one that Kaspian had been desperate to emulate when he'd been a boy. How badly he'd wanted to be just like Henryk, his big brother, who'd turned out to be a monster hiding behind a mask all along. Seeing that smile now... it was like honey laced with poison.

"While I was training at the temple of Perun, Weles came to me in a vision. I was filled with a divine purpose to fulfill his work, to purify this corrupted land, and bring prosperity back to its people." He threw his arms out in a grand gesture, sloshing wine over the rim of his glass in the process, with not a glance at Mama's now wine-stained treasured rug. And then his gaze settled on Kaspian. "Tell me, little brother, have you been touched by misfortune?"

He could see it clearly now. He'd always admired Henryk's charisma, and even now he couldn't help but admire how he twisted such horrors to his own ends.

Kaspian licked his dry lips. "There have been a few unexplained incidents."

Henryk sat up straight and held out his glass for the "disciple" to take before leaning in toward Kaspian. "You see, this is the price you pay for being in the company of witches." Henryk shook his head. "You are young yet, so I can see how her come-hither gaze could have beguiled you. Women, they have it in them, all of them, and only those who submit themselves to Weles and his guidance can ever hope to quell the bit of witch in their nature."

Kaspian straightened and half-rose from his chair while Henryk watched with a single quirked eyebrow. If he exposed his past relationship with Brygida to

Henryk, it could be fuel for his fire, or worse, make her a target. He leaned back in his chair, crossing his legs, but his heart raced. "I don't see how a woman who deals in simple remedies and small magic could be any threat."

Henryk stood up and came close, leaning over Kaspian in his chair. "Oh my dear, sweet Kaspian, you were always too innocent for your own good. If only Tata had lived longer to guide you in rulership."

Henryk put a hand on his shoulder, which he wanted very much to knock away. But he resisted the urge.

"Mama has been guiding me."

Henryk threw his head back and laughed, and his lackeys joined in along with him. "Don't be silly. A woman knows nothing of rulership."

Mama's face flushed. How had he ever seen this man as anything other than an arrogant bastard? Although he had the same blood, this man was not his brother.

Kaspian rose, and Henryk stumbled backward a few steps. "You insult our mother," he said firmly to Henryk, leaning into his space. "Apologize."

Henryk held his gaze with that charismatic smile, but it didn't reach his eyes. No one spoke, no one moved, until finally Mama clearing her throat broke the silence.

With a quick, nonchalant inhalation, Henryk

looked away to Mama, who had her arms wrapped around her torso. "My sincerest apologies, Mama. I spoke too harshly. I'm sure you've done the best you can, given your limited capabilities." His insincere smile broadened as he turned to Kaspian. "But fear not, little brother. I am here now, and I shall help you bring prosperity to the region once more."

He dared? This brazen monster dared insult their mother in her own home?

Was that why he'd come here? To amuse himself with this petty disrespect, while his army watched from the outskirts, ready to destroy them all?

Was that what Henryk wanted? For him to throw the first punch and give Henryk a reason?

"That is very generous of you," Mama said, her voice unusually cheery. "But you and your friends must be tired. Perhaps you would like to rest for a while?"

Henryk's gaze darkened for a moment, and in that split-second, something truly terrifying stirred there. But it was quickly replaced by a smiling mask once more.

"Thank you. I think I would. We have traveled far and wide, spreading Weles's message of peace. A bath would be welcome, and perhaps another bottle of wine." And with that, Henryk strode past them both and out toward the stairs, with a staccato of footsteps as his "disciples" followed after him.

Once those footsteps gave way to silence, Mama exhaled and leaned forward onto her chair.

Kaspian rushed to her, putting a gentle hand on her shoulder. "What can I do to help, Mama?"

It was a stupid question. The one thing that would help would be obliterating Henryk from this life. The one thing he could not do, lest all of Rubin follow at the hands of Henryk's army.

She waved him off. "No, I'm fine, I just... I hoped..." She shook herself. "Don't worry about it." She fixed him with a hard stare and leaned in. "And don't let him bait you. He wants you angry and stupid. Don't give him what he wants, no matter how he provokes you."

She was right.

He'd all but taken the bait, and if not for her intervention, he'd probably be getting flogged in his own courtyard right now. Henryk knew how to prey on love, how to press just hard enough to elicit the reactions he seemed to want.

Even knowing that, however, he wasn't sure he would've been able to react differently, and Henryk had a bounty of loved ones to press here. Doubtless, Henryk was just getting started and, worse, was untouchable.

It was times like this that his hands itched to paint, to work out the swirl of thoughts with oil on canvas. But he'd locked his supplies in a trunk in storage, never to see the light of day.

If he couldn't paint, maybe a walk could help him

clear his head. "I'm going to take some much-needed air," he said to Mama. "Are you going to be all right?"

With a tremulous smile, she nodded. "I believe I'll take a turn in the garden, clear my head a little."

"I'll have Rafał give you a guard detail."

She huffed. "Really, there's no need for—"

He kissed her cheek in parting. "I won't give in on this, so let's pretend you've agreed, and I'll see you later?"

Her lips pinched as if fighting off a smile, she patted his arm. With a final nod, he headed for the courtyard and gave Rafał his orders.

Outside, a boy struggled to get a gaggle of geese back into their pen. Older men watched him struggle, laughing as they gave suggestions on how to capture them.

"Why not help him instead of mocking him?" Kaspian asked one of the watching servants.

The man bowed his head. "Of course, my lord," he said before joining the boy in wrangling the loose geese.

If only help were so simple when it came to handling Henryk and the Cult of Weles. He sighed, looking out past the manor's walls, where his feet wanted to take him. Let them.

Beyond the gate and down along the sunbaked road, he strolled past barren fields where the seeds had yet to break through the dry soil. He breathed in deep, inhaled the earth's musk and the slight sweetness on the spring air, and the necessary essence of these lands he'd never wanted but now couldn't imagine living without. He let it fill him up, all the dark and angry places, until there was nothing in him but Czarnobrzeg, Rubin, Nizina. Home.

In the distance, the blackened trunk of the Perun-struck oak stood against the blooming green of the Madwood it bordered. He should've brought an offering with him, but perhaps Perun would answer his prayers anyway.

As he approached the Perun-struck oak, beneath its shade, Brygida came into view, with her Scythe of the Mother rested against the massive trunk.

He froze in his steps.

Seeing her here, it was like stepping back in time, to when they had first met. She rested one hand on the tree as she stared into the forest, her chestnut hair plaited in that intricate style ladies from Granat often wore.

She hadn't noticed him yet, and maybe it would be better if she didn't. What would he even say to her if she did? When Henryk had invited himself to the manor, she hadn't hidden her disgust. As he bent to Henryk's will, even to spare his people, she couldn't be particularly pleased with him.

He started to back away, but as he did, he stepped on a twig that snapped.

Brygida spun, her violet eyes meeting his as she reached for her vial of lake water.

He put up his hands. "I wasn't expecting to run into you here. Although perhaps I should begin to."

As he lowered his hands, Brygida eyed him uncertainly, her brow creased and her posture guarded. Maybe he should just leave.

"If you're praying, I can come back later." He gestured over his shoulder back toward the manor.

"No, I'm waiting."

"For what?" Or for whom?

With a sigh, she crossed her arms. "Is *he* still there?" She glared in that direction with narrowed eyes, with such malice he'd never seen before.

He cleared his throat. "Yes. He invited himself to stay."

He couldn't look her in the eye; he had to sound like a monster to her. As his gaze skimmed away, it fell on a nest between the boughs. Two red, featherless chicks with large, bulging eyes squawked, and beside them an egg wobbled, a tiny beak struggling to get through the shell.

"And you're all right with that? Allowing him beneath your roof?" Her voice strained.

"No. It's why I had to leave and get some fresh air."

She stepped closer, shaking her head. "Why not just turn him away? Why welcome him into your home?"

He rubbed the back of his neck. It was a fair question. He could lie and say it was all a part of his strategy, but instead the truth came pouring out. "I don't know what to do. I've never won anything against Henryk. I don't know if I'm strong enough, and now the stakes are so much higher."

Brygida said nothing, and he couldn't meet her eyes anyway. The hatching chick broke off a large chunk of its shell, then its little beak pushed through.

Brygida moved into his periphery and just stood with him for a quiet moment. "I don't think you're giving yourself enough credit. You've been through hardships, overcome demons, and your own grief. And he is a man with an army, but..." She tilted her head, and her voice warmed. "He is just a man."

His chest swelled, and he met her gaze again at last. Did she really think that highly of him?

There was a loud squawk, and they looked as one as the third baby chick broke out of its shell at last.

A raven swooped in and landed on the edge of its nest. Enormous, it turned his head this way and that, regarding Brygida and him both with its gleaming shadow eyes.

A smile played on her lips as she met the raven with a matching inquisitive look.

"What is it?" he asked her.

"We shall have to continue this another time," she whispered, her attention entirely on the raven. "My wait is over."

CHAPTER 11

Brygida had been waiting for a sign, and it had appeared, bold as a raven.

Although he raised an eyebrow, Kaspian left her to her solitude. It was time to enter her witch-lands once more and warn her mothers about the Cult of Weles.

She stepped toward the boundary between worlds, but the toe of her boot met a wall like invisible stone. She staggered, her body colliding with the barrier, then fell back, landing hard on her bottom.

Her home rejected her with a message as plain as day: *Unwelcome.*

She rubbed her sore knee, although it didn't hurt nearly as much as the sinking feeling in the pit of her stomach.

She laid her hand on the Perun-struck oak beside her, trying to hear the faintest whisper of the voices of the wood. Just one word, a single flicker of the connection she'd once shared with this land, was all she wanted.

But no matter what she did, their voices remained silent. The wind rustled through the trees. The familiar pathways through the dappled sunlight lay right in front of her. If only she could take a single step forward, or see Mamusia gathering herbs from that patch a few feet away, or Mama hunting rabbits or deer in the brush. Just one glimpse, and she'd be satisfied. It could bolster her until she'd proved herself to Mokosza and could return to her ancestral witchlands once more.

She paced the perimeter of the forest, did everything she could think of to try to reconnect, but the door to home remained shut to her. She clenched her Weles-marked hand.

The raven at its nest cawed and descended to a lower branch, its dark eyes fixed upon her.

She'd been so sure it had been a sign from Mokosza. Maybe its message hadn't been a welcome, but an encouragement to keep trying. She slid down the tree and brought her knees to her chest. "I will be patient."

She had to be. This was her challenge, and the gods moved as They willed. But how would she warn her mothers? She'd let Kaspian leave too soon. At least he could've entered the forest.

Footsteps approached from behind.

She sprang to her feet and reached for the Scythe of the Mother rested against the tree. Not that she could use it for anything more than... well, cutting.

Nina stood back, her eyes wide and focused on the scythe. "I'm sorry. I didn't mean to scare you! I just saw you sitting here, and I thought I would say hello." Nina took a few steps back, her bright-blue dress fluttering in the wind.

Brygida lowered her scythe. "You wanted to say hello to me?" Even after she had killed Dariusz, Nina's father, along with the others at the Mouth of Weles?

Once, she'd thought she could find a friend in Nina, but after Nina had accused Kaspian of murdering Roksana, it had... strained their blossoming friendship. And when she'd had to kill Dariusz and the others to save Mamusia, she'd accepted that friendships with villagers wouldn't be possible.

Nina fidgeted with her apron. "It's been a while, and I never got to properly apologize to you for what happened back then..."

Brygida knitted her eyebrows together. What did one say in these sorts of situations? "*You* wish to apologize to *me*? I believe it is I who should apologize to you."

Nina rubbed her arm. "Oh... I suppose a lot has passed between us, hasn't it?" A faint smile. "I thought, if you'd like, maybe you could come and have tea with my mother and me? I know she'd like to see you."

Her chest tightened. Would Zofia be angry at her for killing her husband? He'd been a wicked man but Nina's father and Zofia's husband nonetheless. It happened sometimes that even beneath the worst abuse, people were traumatized by losing the one who'd hurt them the most.

"You don't have to," Nina quickly added, twirling the tip of her blond braid, "but I've seen you wandering around for a while today. You must be hungry and thirsty."

Before she could protest otherwise, her stomach growled.

Nina smiled and linked arms with her as if it were the most natural thing to do in the world.

Brygida hesitated for a moment. "I'm sorry, but there's something I must do here first."

Nina canted her head and took a step back. "Oh? Is it something I can help with?"

Indeed it was. Like Kaspian, Nina could enter the forest. "I don't suppose you've seen my mothers recently?"

Nina shook her head. "No, not I, but my mother went to tell them about the army. Some of us believe Mokosza's servants are our only hope of sending them away from our borders. We don't want trouble here like there's been in Granat and Szmaragd."

Brygida heaved a sigh of relief. Mokosza's loom,

then Mama and Mamusia had been warned after all, thanks to Zofia. They wouldn't be caught off guard by the cult.

She looked in the direction of the Baran farm. Zofia deserved her thanks. "I would gladly take that tea now, if that's all right?"

Nina raised an eyebrow—why was everyone from the village always making that face at her?—then laughed. "Of course it's all right! Then there isn't something you have to do here?"

Not anymore. "It's done."

Nina eyed the space around her, looked left and right, then shrugged. "This way."

Following Nina's lead, she headed toward the Baran farm through the fields full of plump, grazing dairy cows, their calves frolicking alongside them.

When they approached the house, Zofia carried a load of hay over one shoulder and set it down before dusting her hands off on her breeches. A wide smile broke out across her face. "Oh, we have company. Welcome, Brygida. You two head in. I'll be there in a moment."

A happy glow lit Zofia's face as she took her burden toward the field of cows lingering along the fence line.

Inside, the house looked different than when she had last seen it, airy and bright. A bouquet of irises graced the center of a table, along with scattered papers with charcoal drawings. The drawings depicted vivid, detailed gardens.

"You draw?"

Flushed, Nina gathered up the papers. "Sorry, I should have cleaned these up. My father didn't like it, but now that he's gone, I can design gardens to my heart's content." She beamed, a smile Brygida found herself mirroring. Their farm seemed prosperous, and the two women more carefree. Without the oppressive weight of Dariusz looming over them, they had both blossomed.

Nina pulled the kettle from the fire as Zofia walked in. She kicked off muddy boots before crossing the room and taking Brygida into a tight embrace.

"It is good to see you again," Zofia said, holding her tight.

The hug was unexpected, but not unwanted. Feeling the warm embrace of a mother only made her longing for her own mothers that much keener. "Thank you for warning my mothers. I am most grateful."

Zofia pulled away only enough to nod. "There's nothing to thank me for, truly. When we saw the soldiers arrive, I ran to the Madwood to warn your mothers while Nina ran to the manor house. We'll need our lord and the gods both to save us from this madness." Zofia tsked under her breath, then sighed. "But enough about that. It's been an age since we've seen you, my girl. Where have you been these long months?"

"I was away for a while in Granat." Would it terrify them to know she'd spent the past few months taming demons and trying to reconnect with her lost wrath of the blood? "No Hand of Mokosza tended the witchlands there, so I've been serving."

Nina set a steaming cup of fragrant chamomile tea before Brygida as she and Zofia both took places across from her. "Granat? Is that where that visiting lord is from? The one you arrived with?"

"Yes. He's come to help, if he can." Brygida blew on her tea before taking a sip. "You both seem to be doing well."

Zofia's smile was as broad as her daughter's as she looked around the house. "We've done rather well for ourselves. Without that drunk husband of mine, there have been fewer accidents and the heifers are thriving. We had six calves born this spring."

Brygida acknowledged this with her own smile. It warmed her to see them doing so well. As horrifying as the attack at the Mouth of Weles had been, some good had come of it in the end. If only that dark power could be used for something other than killing.

There was a knock on the door.

Zofia frowned, drawing her arms to her chest. "Who could that be?"

"I'll get it." Nina jumped up and walked over to greet their visitor.

As she walked away, Zofia reached across the table and put her hand on Brygida's. "We cannot thank you enough for all you've done."

She shook her head. It felt wrong to be thanked for killing someone.

"Where is the man of the house?" Henryk's voice demanded.

Brygida stood and reached for her scythe. What was he doing here? But she stepped just out of sight of the doorway. If Henryk learned she was here, he might find a reason to cause trouble for these two women.

Zofia, hands on her hips, joined Nina. "There is no man of the house. Can I help you?"

"I'm sorry to hear that. Are you recently widowed?" He pressed a hand to his chest in mock sympathy, but his eyes were sharp, calculating.

"I don't see how that's any concern of yours," Zofia replied.

"Weles is concerned for all his children." His syrupy smile was enough to make her sick. "I've heard there is a visitor here who's a bad influence." He advanced a step through the doorway.

His gaze slid over to Brygida, and it felt as if she'd been dipped in oil. Would he now cause trouble here over her presence? Or would he dare harm Zofia or Nina? The mark on her palm throbbed again.

If she wanted to, she could summon the demons to her aid and tear him apart. He had come alone, after all.

"I think the only bad influence here is you," Zofia said, holding her ground. "If that's all you came for, I will ask you to leave."

Henryk lurched backward as if he had been struck. Brygida moved closer, putting herself between him and Zofia. If he wanted to toy with her, she'd made certain he'd keep Zofia and Nina out of it.

"As they made clear, you should leave." As the whispers grew louder in her head, Brygida stalked closer. *Kill him. Kill him. Tear him apart*, they urged.

His face twitched, just for a moment, and he backed away with a sniff. "My friends are waiting for me," he said nonchalantly. "I hope I'm not delayed, or they would come searching for me. And they can be a bit overeager in their searches." He gave her a smug smile.

As much as she wanted to kill him, she couldn't. Not with an army of misguided souls waiting on the outskirts.

Just by standing up for Zofia and Nina, she had likely put a target on their backs. "If you have no business with them, perhaps you should leave."

"Oh, but there is still business to attend to. This young woman is without a suitor." He gave Nina a slow once-over, lingering over her chest. "She should join my disciples. Such a shame to waste youth in such a way, when she could be serving... Weles." He approached

Nina, who trembled, her eyes wide as he reached for her cheek.

"I would appreciate it if you didn't put a hand on my betrothed," Kaspian said from behind him, panting in the doorway, his hand at the hilt of his sword. His face so reddened, he must have run here.

Without a glance at Brygida, he approached Nina and took her hand in his.

Seeing their hands intertwined filled her stomach with hot coals. Was he just protecting Nina, or had he moved on already? Brygida stiffened but restrained the intensity of her emotions. There were more important things at stake here than her feelings: two lives.

"You two are engaged?" Henryk raised an incredulous eyebrow.

"We are, and I would thank my brother kindly to not insult my future bride." Kaspian faced Henryk with an unwavering gaze. Nothing in the room dared move, dared sound.

Finally, Henryk smirked. "I see, well, congratulations, little brother. I hope I can stay long enough to bless your upcoming nuptials."

"I'm sure you'll be too busy for that. Your followers came looking for you at the manor."

"Ah, I suppose I shall be returning, then." He tipped his head to Nina. "Sister." Then with one last lingering stare for Brygida, he strode away.

That cur of a man. He had followed her here; she

was certain of it. His game seemed to rely on manipulating those she cared about.

But if he tried to hurt them... he'd regret it.

⚜

It was fortunate Kaspian had tracked Henryk to the Baran farm. If he hadn't arrived in time, what might've happened? He shuddered at the thought. Still, he hadn't had much time to think before he'd declared Nina his betrothed. He would have to clear up any misunderstandings before they could lead to more.

"May I talk to you for a moment?" Kaspian asked Nina.

She looked at him with a furrowed brow, but thank Perun she hadn't questioned him in front of Henryk. "Yes?"

He'd tried to protect her in one way, but in another, he might have made her a target.

"I should probably go as well." Brygida lifted up her scythe, and before he could stop her, she headed out the door and toward the forest. He followed her out, Nina's hand still in his, but as he stood outside, he realized he couldn't let go. Not until Henryk was far, far away.

Instead, he stood there, frozen to the spot, watching Brygida's form disappear into the distance while he held another woman's hand.

For her part, Nina remained silent until he faced her.

"Sorry. I must have surprised you." He rubbed the back of his neck as Nina eyed their joined hands.

"It was unexpected, but I'm not sure what he would have done had you not arrived when you did." The color still hadn't returned to her cheeks. As awkward as this was for him, it had to be equally so for her, if not more. She, too, had someone she cared for.

"I'd appreciate it if you didn't bring this up to Stefan." The last thing he wanted was for Stefan to think he was after his lover. "I'll talk to him about it."

"Stefan?" Nina tilted her head. "Why would I tell him?"

Kaspian cleared his throat. He knew that they were keeping their relationship a secret, but now that he knew, surely they could be truthful? "I've seen him headed to your farm quite frequently lately."

Nina's eyes were wide as she put one hand over her mouth. And just like that, color did begin to return to her cheeks. "Oh, yes. Well, thank you."

When he released her hand, she bobbed her head and scurried back toward the house without another word. Had he said something wrong? Perhaps Nina and Stefan preferred to keep their relationship a secret still?

With a heavy sigh, he turned back toward the manor. Something had to be done about Henryk, but how could he get him out of town without the inquisitors and the army destroying the village?

As he made his way down the path from the Baran farm, he spotted Henryk leaning against a fence. In his hand was a branch with fresh buds that had yet to bloom, and without looking at them, Henryk snapped off small pieces from the end. Henryk never could sit still; he was always moving.

Henryk raised his chin, then straightened. He dumped the shredded remnants of the branch onto the ground and strolled over to him. Head held high, he wore that infuriatingly smug look on his face.

"You didn't need to wait for me. Your messenger will be anxious," Kaspian said as he approached him.

"They can wait a few more moments. I was hoping to see what hole that witch slunk off to." Henryk craned his neck, as if scanning the horizon, searching for her.

Was Henryk doing this just to get a rise out of him? Whatever the motives, he needed to tread carefully here. "You never told me what you were doing at the Baran farm."

Henryk's blue eyes flickered toward him, studying his face for a moment before he shrugged. "That witch is dangerous. She will only continue corrupting this region, brother. Women aren't meant to wander like that."

Kaspian clenched his jaw so hard he thought that he might crack a tooth. "Is that so?"

Henryk watched the forest again. "Remember this when you make that girl your wife. They need a husband to beat them or their liver will rot. Don't let that witch's influence corrupt her and give her ideas that she is in charge. It's bad enough you've let our mother tell you what to do..."

He was going to punch Henryk in his petulant mouth. His fist was ready.

Myriad shouts came from the manor house.

In the distance, a crowd gathered outside the gates. Had the peasants started to revolt already? Had Henryk's cult already converted so many?

Leaving Henryk behind, Kaspian bolted toward the crowd, his heart thundering in his chest. The last time he'd gone against a mob, they'd almost separated him from his manhood, but this time he wouldn't hesitate.

"Out of my way!" he roared, elbowing his way through the crowd until he reached the front. At the head, Agata wielded her cleaver, swinging it in the air.

"We've come for the rapist!" she snarled, her face contorted with rage.

The crowd chanted. "Give him up! Give him up!"

Henryk. They wanted Henryk.

Word of his arrival must have already spread. But if he turned Henryk over to the mob now, there was no telling what the cult army would do. They could disband, or... they could come to the village and kill everyone. As much as it galled him, he'd have to keep

Henryk alive until Lord Granat could arrive with his forces.

Rafał was closing in with his guards, glancing over here for orders.

"If you have a grievance," Kaspian called, "I would ask you to present it at the next hearing."

"There is no justice here. You will pardon him, as your father did before you!" Agata shouted wild eyed.

"If you do not disperse, you will leave me no choice but to use force." Kaspian nodded toward the guards, who advanced.

But instead of dispersing as he hoped they would, the mob turned and fought the guards. Voices rang out, cries and yells and screams.

Kaspian reached for his sword as a nearby peasant lunged for him. He didn't want to draw the blood of his own people.

"Men, to me!" Kaspian roared, but a hand grasped him and pulled him from the fray. Brygida, holding her scythe at the ready.

Some heads turned to look at her, but only for a moment as punches landed and swords met pitchforks.

"My people!" Henryk's booming voice rang out.

As one, the people who watched stilled.

"You!" Agata pointed her cleaver at him and pushed her way to the front of the crowd. "I will make you pay for what you did to my daughter!"

The crowd behind her roared in approval.

But as she approached, five women in black stepped in front of Henryk, blocking her. And when she tried to push her way through, they pushed her back.

"I know you came here seeking justice, but your anger is unfounded," Henryk said with a smile. "You know me. I was once a member of this community. Loved by many. You, Leopold—who helped you when your ox was in a ditch?"

"You," said Leopold, hesitantly.

"And you, Olga, when your husband died before the harvest, who brought men to help you and save you from starving that winter?" Henryk asked, pointing at her.

Olga lowered her head. "It was you, my lord."

One by one, he called out to people in the crowd, until slowly they calmed, lowering their weapons. What was this charisma? How could Henryk be this manipulative?

"It doesn't matter what you've done in the past! It doesn't change that you raped my daughter," Agata said as she struggled.

Henryk sighed. "I will admit, your daughter and I were lovers."

"Then you admit it!" Agata hissed.

Henryk shook his head. "I would never force myself upon a woman. Do I look as though I would need to?" He smiled and winked at the women around him. A few of them blushed.

It was enough to make Kaspian's stomach turn. Henryk really could convince people the blue sky was green.

"We were lovers, it is true, and your daughter did not want you to find out that we had shared a bed before marrying. I would have married her, but the gods called me to their service." He lowered his head. "And before I left, I made sure she had enough to support herself and to live a good life without me. But I can see your greed, Agata, has not ceased. Because your daughter did not marry well, you would dare to slander my name?"

There were murmurs amongst the crowd as they shared looks amongst themselves.

They couldn't be believing this, could they?

It was on the tip of his tongue to condemn Henryk as Agata did, but he had to be smarter than he'd been before. It would be the right thing to do to support Agata here, but the right thing would get her killed. And him. And the crowd. That thought, as true as it was, slithering in his head like a vile serpent.

He couldn't move against Henryk until he had Lord Granat's army to protect his people from the cult's reprisals.

Until then, he had to stall.

"It is clear to me how the corruption of morals in this village has led you all to lust for violence," Henryk lectured. "But please look upon yourselves, think of your abandoned fields that need planting, the livestock that needs tending. Wouldn't your time be better spent on your own farms than here, making false accusations against an innocent man?"

They muttered to themselves, and one by one, the crowd began to disperse. Only Agata lingered.

She spat on the ground in front of him. "You will pay for what you did. Mark my words."

"Go, Agata. I forgive you for your greed." Henryk gestured toward the road.

Without her mob behind her, surrounded by inquisitors, she retreated. The guards followed the crowd of villagers to make sure they didn't return.

And just like that, Henryk had evaded justice yet again. And who had stood by and allowed it to happen?

His blood curdled like sludge in his veins. He shuddered and shook his head. His silence had spared the blood of his people, but why did it have to feel so wrong?

If he'd only spoken out, it would've felt right. It would've brought to light something dark and evil. But instead, he'd stayed silent out of worry, out of fear. For survival.

Brygida, who had been holding his hand all that time, was clenching it hard enough to crush his bones.

Henryk turned toward them, with a small smirk pulling at his lips upon seeing their clasped hands. Brygida pulled away.

"You see, brother? You need a firm hand with these people."

A bitter taste in his mouth, Kaspian watched the dispersing crowd.

"It's good that I'm here, Kaspian, to protect you from all manner of ill things."

Ill things?

Henryk's gaze fixed on Brygida.

CHAPTER 12

Brygida did not sleep at all that night. Every time she tried to close her eyes, the slightest creak of floorboards or the whisper of wind on the windows had her jolting up, expecting to find the Dog of Weles or his inquisitors pinning her down to the bed.

With her scythe close by at all times, it gave her some comfort but not nearly enough. If she wanted, she could summon the demons to her aid, but every time her thoughts strayed that way, the immense loss of life at the Mouth of Weles returned, vivid as if it had happened only yesterday. The bodies in the snow, black ooze trailing from every facial orifice... There had to be another way to stop the Dog of Weles.

At last, sunlight fell through the curtains. A single shaft of light illuminated the otherwise dark room, and there was no use trying to sleep anymore. She swung her legs out of bed.

The cold floor sent a chill up her spine, so she dressed quickly before heading out into the hall. She needed to talk to Nikodem; maybe he had another plan to stop Henryk.

Her room was close to the kitchen, and the smell of smoke and ash filled her nostrils. The household had just started lighting the fires for the day and it was early yet, so perhaps she could get out of the manor without being seen. The only reason she hadn't tried sleeping outdoors was because she knew she'd be safer within four walls. But while the Dog of Weles remained in residence here, she wouldn't stay another moment longer.

As Brygida hurried down the hall, Lady Rubin stood on the other end of it, elegantly coiffed and clad in an evergreen dress, talking with the servants. She glanced at Brygida and waved her over.

It would be rude to just keep walking, as much as she wanted to. With a slow bob of her head, Brygida approached.

"You're up early," Lady Rubin said with a smile.

Since she'd arrived, Lady Rubin had been very kind, a stark contrast to the woman she had been when Brygida had come during Kolęda.

"I often rise with the sun," Brygida remarked.

Lady Rubin nodded. "There's always too much to do, and never enough sunlight." She shook her head and cleared her throat delicately. "Are your mothers well?"

As much as Brygida tried to avoid the topic of her mothers, the reminders were everywhere, although Lady Rubin probably hadn't meant to hurt her with the question. "I haven't seen them in months."

"Oh." Lady Rubin pressed a hand to her chest. "I'm sorry to hear that. Is everything all right?"

So very little was all right, but she couldn't explain losing Mokosza's favor and what that meant to a Mrok witch. "I haven't been able to visit them yet." Which was true enough.

A slight flush colored Lady Rubin's pale cheeks.

"Is something wrong?"

Lady Rubin glanced around. "Oh yes, well this is a rather delicate topic... Could we possibly speak somewhere more private?"

Brygida quirked a brow, but she had seen this sort of look on a woman's face. A woman with secrets, a woman who did not want others to know. "Yes, we can."

Lady Rubin led her up the stairs to a small dark room with a gray-blanketed bed and the curtains drawn. The fire had not yet been built, and a cold draft left it with a chill. Lady Rubin paced back and forth a bit. "I don't know where to start."

"Your secrets are safe with me. Are you with child? How far?" Brygida asked.

Lady Rubin's head popped up. "Oh dear, no." She shook her head again and laughed. "It's nothing like that. My, you are kind to think... Anyway, that is not important right now. I wanted to speak with you about my son."

Kaspian. Would Lady Rubin tell her to stay away from him? Her gut twisted. "I can assure you, I have no intention of interfering in Kaspian's life."

Lady Rubin blinked a few times. "Kaspian..." Her eyelashes fluttered downward. "I must admit, I was wrong to interfere between the two of you. He hasn't been the same since you left. He's glum, quiet. He's stopped painting."

Kaspian without a brush in his hand? She couldn't imagine it. "Why would he stop painting?"

Lady Rubin wrung her hands together. "He says he needs to focus on being a lord, but every day, I see my son fading away, more and more..." Lady Rubin shook her head and took a deep breath. "But Kaspian is not why I asked to speak with you. It's about my older son, Henryk."

Brygida tensed. "What about him?"

Lady Rubin took a step closer, her face lined, hardened. "I want you to make him pay for what he did."

Brygida's mouth fell open. She couldn't have heard her correctly. This woman had once come to pay off her mothers when she'd thought Kaspian guilty of rape and murder. What had changed her mind?

"Why?" Brygida asked. "Not that he doesn't deserve to pay, but why now?"

Lady Rubin took another shaking breath. "When Henryk attacked that poor girl, I sent him away not just to protect him and the women of the village, but I thought—no, I hoped he could find redemption through serving Perun. I tried to pretend I didn't see the darkness in him, the anger and resentment he had held inside. But seeing him now, serving this cult... I cannot keep turning the other way. He has to pay for what he's done."

Then they were of the same mind. "I will see him pay, no matter what. I swear this."

Shouts came from downstairs.

Exchanging a look with Lady Rubin, she ran to the top of the stairs. Kaspian emerged from his study, in the same rumpled clothes as the day before. He looked as if he hadn't slept.

"Gather the guards!" he ordered a servant, then grabbed a man by the arm. "Make sure we have people posted along the roads in case the villagers riot."

Brygida raced down the stairs and hurried over to him. "What's going on?"

"It's Agata." He turned bloodshot eyes to her. "Her body was found this morning by the forest's edge."

Brygida shook her head.

It couldn't be true; she had just seen Agata the day before.

Kaspian put his hand on her shoulder.

If Agata was dead, there could only be one culprit. "Your brother did this, to silence her."

His lips were drawn in a thin line. "I fear you're right."

She would kill Henryk. She would tear him apart. For what he had done to Agata, who had done nothing more than speak the truth, for the sake another innocent woman whose life had been cut too short...

To avenge women killed at the hands of men—this was the Mokosza's holiest order. This was what it meant to serve as Her Hand. As Her Reaper of Death.

But... she was no longer the Reaper here.

If Agata had been murdered by a man, that meant Mamusia would be called to Reap Agata's killer.

A chill ran down Brygida's spine. There was no doubt in her mind that Henryk had played a role in Agata's murder, if not done it with his own hands, but did he also hope to lure out Mamusia with this? To hurt her?

Would Mamusia expect to be attacked by female inquisitors?

Brygida's heart raced, and a dark hole haunted by a witch's dying scream shrouded her vision. The Mouth of Weles in Granat. Had this been how Anita had been flushed out, to be murdered by the Cult of Weles?

Not here. Not again. Never again.

She had to find Mamusia. Without another word to

Kaspian, she ran out of the manor and down the road. As she ran, she kept glancing toward the forest, hoping for a glimpse of Mamusia. Closer to the village square, more people crowded the roads, both inquisitors and villagers.

The inquisitors clustered around the well, their gazes trained on the edge of the forest. The Dog of Weles was nowhere to be seen. This was a trap set for Mamusia. She had to warn her somehow.

Diving behind a building, she circumvented the crowd and made her way closer to the forest, minding the edge. Shadows and trees hid anything from view, and the pounding of her heart filled her ears.

Mamusia stepped out from amid the new ferns.

Garbed in the ceremonial white robes, sashed with the red Belt of the Golden Spider, and carrying the Mrok Scythe of the Mother, it was both Mamusia and not. It was the woman she knew as mother, and every Mrok witch of her line.

Mamusia strode toward the village, her head held high and her waves of golden hair flowing behind her. Seeing her again, Brygida's heart swelled, and although Mamusia was doing her holy duty, she could not stop her feet from running toward Mamusia, tears streaming down her face.

As she ran, Mamusia's violet eyes widened, her arms open, and she wrapped Brygida into her embrace.

The comforting lavender and chamomile scent of

Mamusia, the circle of her arms, was enough to make her weep for joy. She wanted to cry on Mamusia's shoulder as she had when she'd been a little girl, to lay all her burdens at her mother's feet.

"Brygida, my Brygida. You've returned to us. Have you repaid your debt already?" Mamusia's eyes brimmed with tears.

Brygida wiped away her own. "Not yet. I came to give you a warning. I know who killed Agata. He's from the Cult of Weles, and I think he's set a trap to lure you here."

Please, Holy Mokosza, I beg you. Protect her. Please. Please...

Mamusia lifted her head and scanned the crowd. The gathered villagers watched, and the inquisitors had moved in front of them.

"I see." A rumble of power thundered in Mamusia's voice, one she'd so rarely heard. A flash lit her stormy gaze.

"It would seem this village has an infestation of witches." Henryk emerged from among the crowd, and the inquisitors fell into place behind him.

Brygida put herself between him and Mamusia, but Henryk's eyes lingered on Mamusia and a smile quirked at the corner of his mouth.

The mark on her hand throbbed, at first a faint pulse that gradually became thunder, a painful thunder, lined with the whispers of demons.

Their voices filled her up, storm clouds consuming the sky of her mind, drowning out nearly all other sounds. *Tear him apart, limb from limb... Let the dark power consume them and destroy them all...*

She wouldn't let them lay a hand on Mamusia again.

But there were innocents here. Too many lives would be lost if she lost control now.

Mamusia put her hand on Brygida's shoulder and stepped in front of her. Not a sound dared hinder her movement. "I come on Mokosza's business for one of Her fallen. Would you stand in Her way?"

At the front of his line of inquisitors, Henryk faced her with that faint smile of his, sickly sweet like the stench of dead flesh. He let the moment drag on a little too long before that sickly sweet smile broadened. "Weles is Her consort. I would never interfere in Her work."

With that, he moved aside, as did the rest of the crowd, letting Mamusia stride past them toward the Duma Inn.

Huddled together in the doorway, the stoic innkeeper and his daughter, Dorota, awaited. Mamusia reached them, letting one of the red yarns from the Belt of the Golden Spider pass over her fingers before cutting it and handing it to them sadly.

Agata's widower accepted it with a large, quivering

palm, where its length hung limply for a moment before he closed his hand around it.

Villagers bowed their heads, offered their sympathies, and Mamusia nodded solemnly to them both. The innkeeper held his daughter close, and they took Agata's red yarn inside.

People slowly began to disperse, but Mamusia lingered at the door, head bowed. Brygida approached her and clasped her hand. This couldn't be easy for Mamusia. None of this.

"I saw it in my dreams, but I didn't want to believe it," Mamusia said softly. "This will not be a simple Reaping." She shook her head. "I fear... I fear—"

"I can help. We will find a way to bring him to justice." Brygida gave Mamusia's hand a squeeze.

Mamusia caressed her cheek. "You've grown so much."

Brygida leaned into her touch, didn't want to let her go. Despite everything that was happening around them, with Mamusia here, it somehow felt safer, as it always had. But even with Mamusia's reassurances, they still had only three days to bring the Dog of Weles to justice, or it would be Mamusia who would pay the rusałki's price. A Mrok witch who failed in her duties as Reaper of Death would be dragged into Mroczne Lake by the rusałki, to become one of them.

She had narrowly avoided the depths during Julian's Reaping for Roksana's murder, and she wouldn't let

Mamusia suffer that terrible fate. No, Henryk would pay.

A figure in a white tabard approached on horseback, a man-at-arms in Rubin's uniform. Mamusia stepped in front of her, scythe held out before them.

The man's horse reared backward, and he struggled to get the mount under control once more. "Brygida Mrok of the Madwood, Lord Rubin requires your help. Demons are attacking."

Mokosza's great loom... Demons, here? Did that mean—

Mamusia put her hand on her shoulder. "The forest is waking. Go. I can handle the rest."

The man offered her a hand, and she swung into the saddle with him before they raced out to the farms.

CHAPTER 13

U rging Demon into a canter, Kaspian led a squad of guards toward the dark cloud of smoke invading the twilit sky. Ten would be enough. They'd have to be enough. Perun willing, the messenger had reached Brygida swiftly, and she'd already arrived. Demons were her preserve, and she could save the Baran farm. She could.

Or else he and his guards would have to do. First Agata's murder, and now this...

With Stefan and his guards at his back, they rode up to the Baran house. In the yard, Zofia wielded a garden hoe while Nina held a pitchfork, both of them bloody and sweat soaked.

Stefan was already on the ground sprinting toward them when Kaspian swung down from the saddle and approached. "Are you both all right?"

"We're fine, but our herd isn't. They're almost all dead. We were only able to save one pregnant heifer." Tears streaming down her face, Zofia jutted out her chin.

"I'll help you both. You don't need to worry." Kaspian put a reassuring hand on Zofia's shoulder.

"Thank you, my lord. I will find a way to repay your kindness somehow."

Nina looked to Stefan and then to her mother, herself on the brink of tears. And he didn't blame her—in a single afternoon, they'd lost everything. After all their hard work, to have it all stolen from them was too cruel.

"Can you show us the herd?" His experience with demons was limited, but he would try to get an idea of what they were up against, at least.

Zofia and Stefan shared a look that Kaspian couldn't interpret, before she gestured toward the field with her garden hoe. Where just the day before there had been cows grazing on fresh green shoots, now there were bloodied mounds, white bones sticking out of the mangled carcasses in a muddy field.

Kaspian walked carefully among the mangled corpses, his stomach turning. He'd come face to face with demons before, and considering the brutal way these animals had been torn apart, there was no doubt in his mind a demon had caused it.

A head-splitting scream rent the air.

FALL OF THE REAPER

Kaspian drew his sword.

From the forest came a large creature, horse like in shape, but its mane and tail overflowed like ripe ears of oats, and rows of sharp teeth lined its mouth. It wasn't coming toward him and his men, but peered at Nina and Stefan with its gleaming red eyes.

He was too far away, but he had to try. He took off at a sprint, rushing toward them to help.

Stefan grabbed Nina by the hand and pulled her away, but his boots kept sinking into the mud. The guards rushed in, but in the mud they wouldn't get there in time.

Stefan and Nina would be trampled, or worse.

From out of the right field, a horse came rushing in, and on its back behind a guard was Brygida.

"No, don't!" Brygida shouted.

A guard swung his sword at the demon.

She held a hand up in the air, wreathed in black ether.

The demon barreled toward her. Tendrils of black mist surrounded it and it breathed in that dark air until it wrenched backward.

Stumbling, the demon at last raised its head, but it did not move further.

Brygida dismounted and approached it, her hand lifted, and still, the demon did not move. It would attack her, wouldn't it? Try to hurt her? His feet hadn't stopped moving, and he rushed toward her and the demon, but it...

It remained still. Uncertain.

Stefan helped Nina to safety among the guards as the demon backed away from Brygida, rearing its head and roaring in her direction.

Kaspian approached, his sword drawn. If she needed his help, he'd be close.

"Stay back." Brygida's voice rang with power. But this was different than what he'd glimpsed in her before; it was harsher, darker.

The demon paced before her as she drew ever closer, and once she stood in front of the demon, it bowed to her—or he was pretty sure it was a bow.

Brygida and the demon stared at one another for a few moments before the demon dipped its horse-like head and turned back toward the forest. She traced its retreat with a firm look, her marked hand clad in black smoke.

When she turned back to him again, her expression went slack. He wanted to offer her a shoulder to lean upon, an arm around her waist... Instead, he rubbed his jaw. "That was amazing. How did you get the demon to leave?"

As the smoke faded, she rubbed the black mark on her palm. "I used my Mark of Weles to tame it. The forest is waking because your brother murdered Agata on our witchlands."

The way she said *your brother* felt like a slap to the face.

"I'm on your side, Brygida. Don't you know that?"

She took a deep breath, holding her chin high, stiff. "He's after my mother. He saw her in the square when she came as the Reaper of Death."

The way she said it, measured and calm, held back too much. A shiver rode up his spine; if she feared showing her true thoughts on the matter, veneered them with calm, then she had to be terrified.

If Liliana had taken on the role as Reaper, it meant a life would be over, either hers or Henryk's—there could be no compromise. The time for that was over. He'd tried, and now Agata was dead. "I understand. I will do whatever is necessary."

She met his gaze for a moment, then looked back to the forest. "As I was leaving, the Cult of Weles was assembling in the square. I don't know what they're doing, but you'd be wise to find out."

The cult already schemed while his and Brygida's attention had turned elsewhere. Henryk had to have known about the destruction here, but rather than coming to Zofia and Nina's aid, he'd seized the opportunity to pursue his secret agenda. More lies and deception.

Kaspian mounted up and urged Demon toward the direction of the village square, but Brygida broke away on her own horse she'd borrowed from the guard.

He frowned. "Aren't you coming?"

"There's something else I have to do," she called back. "But I'll join you as soon as I can. By Her thread, Kaspian."

"By Her thread," he whispered, as she rode away toward the forest. He wanted to ask her what was more important than the cult's misdeeds in the village, but as he departed with his guards, the question crumbled away.

If Brygida was leaving when she was needed, then she had something crucial to do. He knew that now, and should've always known it, but he'd been too blind to see it. And Nikodem had benefited from that myopia.

With a deep breath, he shook his head clear. He'd have to win the village and the peasants among the cult to his side on his own if Brygida didn't return in time...

...Or else he'd have to draw his blade against the serpent soon. Far too soon.

CHAPTER 14

A s Kaspian neared Czarnobrzeg's village square, its usual sight of cambered, stone-paved space was saturated with people—black-cloaked cultists, colorfully garbed peasants, and now his white-tabard guards. Whatever Henryk had schemed, it had brought out nearly the entire village, as well as those who'd come with the cult.

"Surround them. We will subdue them peacefully if we can," Kaspian instructed Rafał as he swung down from Demon's saddle. A sea of backs faced him, and at their center Henryk stood upon the edge of the well.

Nikodem and his guards sidled up to Kaspian, and Nikodem leaned in. "My father's leading the united forces here, and they're within a few hours," he murmured. "I'll ride to meet them and fill in my father on the new developments."

This was it. The timing finally coming together.

Kaspian gave a nod, and Nikodem disappeared with his men.

Henryk's black cloak billowed in the wind. His inquisitors flanked him, in their high-collared gowns and the silver horned serpent pins on their chests. Kaspian slowly made his way through the crowd, sliding between the press of bodies and keeping his head down so as to not alert Henryk too soon.

"The witches were said to be our protectors, keeping us safe against demons and all the evil we were told we cannot fight." Henryk paused and Kaspian chanced a glimpse. Henryk scanned the crowd, meeting the gazes of those assembled before him. It was one of Henryk's specialties; even in a crowd of people, he always made sure to make everyone feel as if they were having an intimate conversation.

"And yet here in my own home, demons terrorize you, my friends and neighbors. Your crops are failing, your livestock are dead, and worse yet, a demon has murdered one of us." Henryk threw his arms out as if to embrace the entire crowd.

Sympathetic murmurs rippled through the people. How dare he use Agata's death to twist the truth? And worse, the crowd agreed with him.

Kaspian searched for his guards, their white clothes pale dots amongst a sea of colors, but as they moved through the crowd, people he didn't recognize impeded their way, perhaps disguised cultists strategically placed amongst the villagers. The Cult of Weles was doing everything in its power to block his guards from getting to the front. They scuffled, drawing the attention of the villagers, who came to the guards' aid.

"We were sold a lie!" Henryk raised both hands as his voice reached a fever pitch.

All around him, the peasants shouted, led by the cultists in disguise, who shouted the loudest and swayed the crowd.

"The witches don't protect us—they're allied with the demons!" Henryk shouted.

"That's right!" a cultist in the crowd shouted.

"I've seen it! One of them was summoning a demon with her blood," called out another cultist.

"And they lure innocent men to murder them!" shouted another voice.

They were everywhere, surrounding him, wearing the masks of friends, farmers, and farmhands. Some were from Czarnobrzeg, and others he'd never seen before in his life. This was how they turned people against their better judgment, by planting pretenders in the crowd, using the community against itself.

Henryk held up his hands to silence them. "I have heard your fears and concerns many times. But fear not, we can stop them." He gestured to the inquisitors, who stood beside him like dark shadows, their expressions devoid of all emotion but for the mad glint in their eyes.

"Help us!" Voices rose up.

"Save us!"

"Anything to be rid of the witches!"

Henryk had spewed enough rhetoric. The guards had subdued those who would sabotage them in the crowd, but their numbers had only been halved; it might not be enough. Across the way, Rafał met his gaze.

It was now or never.

Kaspian nodded and moved to the front of the crowd. As he approached, Henryk met his gaze, and for a moment, something truly mad flashed in his eyes, but quickly smoothed over.

Henryk looked back to the people. "We will fight for you," he yelled, "but we cannot do this alone! We need all of you, brothers and sisters, to join us in removing this plague upon our community!"

Now or never. Now or never. Now or never...

"You claim the witches are the cause of our recent problems? How is that possible?" Kaspian challenged, shouting loud enough so his voice carried.

Henryk's eyebrows knitted together in a semblance of gravity. "As Weles's chosen, I was given a vision. In it, our great and powerful Weles revealed to me the darkness and wickedness of the witches, and I was charged with purifying and saving the people from their depravity."

"The witches have always been in Czarnobrzeg and

we have prospered," Kaspian called back, earning nods and murmurs of agreement. "Our land was peaceful and our harvests plenty."

A ripple of chatter went through the crowd, but not enough. Too many kept their ears closed to the truth. He would have to drive the point home.

Kaspian stood before the crowd, his back to Henryk. "In fact, we didn't start seeing blighted crops and demons coming from the forest until the Cult of Weles arrived." Turning, he met Henryk's blazing glare.

"It is clear why you would come to the defense of the witches, little brother," Henryk replied, a gleam in his eyes. "You've been beguiled by them, as so many have before you. Do not fall for the lies of these temptresses! Although they pretend to be human, they are demons in disguise, filled with wickedness and immorality."

Kaspian shook his head vehemently. "You all *know* the Mrok witches! Brygida has walked among you as the Reaper. She found the man who killed my betrothed, Roksana. And Brygida's mother before her has punished those who would raise a hand against women. And who among the women of this village has not had Ewa tend to their childbirth, their loved ones' death rites, or sought her for a remedy?"

The women in the crowd shared looks and slow nods. It was working. They were seeing the light. The guards were in position on either side of Henryk.

"You, Henryk, should have paid for the crimes you committed. And now, I shall see you punished. Capture him."

The guards pushed forward, but the inquisitors in black rushed to block Henryk from view. As the two sides struggled against one another, the crowd joined them, pulling back the inquisitors and giving the guards a straight path to grasp Henryk.

"Arrest him," Kaspian said.

But before his guards could grab a hold of him, more cultists surged forward, cutting off the guards' path and protecting Henryk.

"It's already too late." Henryk didn't move from his place at the edge of the fountain, a smirk on his face. "The lord of Rubin needs to be saved from the witches' manipulation, and Rubin needs to be saved from their evil." Henryk's blue eyes bored into his. "I already gave the order to rid this place of the witches in Weles's name, and burn the Madwood."

BRYGIDA STOOD IN THE SHADE OF THE PERUN-STRUCK oak, facing the trees. Night was falling beyond the horizon, and long shadows stretched, reaching across the landscape.

Shadows and light interplayed with one another, Mokosza's gift and the Mark of Weles. If she hadn't possessed this mark, then Nina might have died to the demon, an *owsiany koń*, an oats horse demon the guard had regretfully angered.

And yet, she still couldn't return to the home her heart longed for. But just as the light illuminated the day, the moon and stars guided the nights. Perhaps dark and light weren't as singular as she had thought.

Matoha approached from her side, swishing his long tail. *You still long to return?*

She ignored him and turned away from the forest.

You may never regain what is lost to you. But if you embrace your god-gifted powers, it might be enough to save them all.

She faced Matoha. "You can taunt me all you want, but I am never going to give up." She spun on her heel and marched away from him. From the day she'd met Matoha in Anita's witchlands, he had been nothing but a pain. All he wanted was to tempt her down a dark path.

Even if she couldn't enter the forest, there had to be a way she could stop it from waking. It was restless, and she could feel it without communing with it, but not completely awake, not yet.

Demons were coming, and for now, the least she could do was try to tame those that woke.

Concentrating on her mark, she listened to the voices of the demons who had followed her here from Anita's witchlands. Their voices, at first, were a cacophony that made her skull throb. But focusing on the sounds, she was able to discern their individual voices. There, among the farmhouses, a demon hunted, a cub-like *panek* clawing at the wall of a house.

She would start with him. Brygida jumped into the saddle and followed the trail to a far-off hut.

When she arrived, a pack of demons circled it, scratching at the oaken door. She dismounted, and one of the *panki* turned toward her, a small ursine creature with fearsome claws and teeth. Matoha was there, too; she hadn't even realized he'd followed her.

If you win them to your side, they will fight for you. They will save this village.

She clutched her scythe. She'd tamed many demons and had tried to fight even more. And no matter how hard she tried, they kept on coming. What if Matoha was right? What if the only way to defeat these monsters was to embrace the power within her?

A *panek* stalked closer, and inside the hut, people screamed. She had to lure them away, and one was already on her trail.

The *panki* followed their pack mate and closed in around her. They thought her easy prey, maybe, but little did they know, she was not alone. And she did not plan to go quietly. With a hand raised, she summoned the many demons who had followed her, drawing them in.

The panki leaped at her. She jumped out of the way of the gnashing teeth.

Out of the forest came the lichyj she had tamed. It charged into the panki, scattering them. They turned, their attention divided between Brygida and the demons.

Call them to you. You have that power.

And it was thrumming through her like a second heartbeat, their voices filling her head in the way the whispers of her ancestors had once spoken to her through the Scythe of the Mother. They were a part of her; they were Weles's blessing. These demons that she'd seen as an inconvenience, a burden that had followed her around.

Gathering up her strength, she reached outward, further than she had ever done before. The Mark of Weles throbbed, and black smoke spilled out from inside of it.

Hear me, demons, and obey my call. Her own voice echoed through her mind. And all the demons fighting before her turned as one, their eyes trained on her. She was doing it, controlling them all.

This was it.

This was how she would protect her mothers and the village.

Good. Now you must move quickly, Matoha said. *The women in black, they are in the forest with fire.*

Her chest clenched. Mama and Mamusia... she had to get to them.

The horse she had ridden here danced and shied away, bolting from the demons. There was no time to waste trying to go after it. Matoha approached her and knelt on the ground before her.

"You want me to ride you?"

Matoha blinked crimson eyes at her.

There was no time to question it. She climbed on his back, and as soon as she grasped onto a tuft of fur on his neck, they were speeding across the countryside.

From a distance, a red glow began to burn against the twilit sky. The screams of the forest pierced her skull and nearly knocked her off Matoha's back.

The forest was waking. The cultists were committing evil deeds, enough to wake the witchlands.

How dare they! Rage boiled inside her. As she rushed to the forest's edge, Matoha reared. He would move no further.

"What are you doing? My mothers need me. We have to go in there."

You cannot. Someone else must go in your place.

Still. She was still fallen of Mokosza.

Her mark throbbed. The forest was all that separated her from the cult as they closed in on her family. Neither Mama nor Mamusia could commune with demons, so she couldn't send one to them. Who could possibly go in her place to warn her mothers?

She turned her gaze back to the village. "Take me to Kaspian."

Matoha bowed his head, and they raced back toward the manor, over fields cast in long shadows and the dying light of day. People rushed around with panicked, hasty steps, and amid all the desperate activity, she found Kaspian with a group of guards, sitting in the saddle, giving hasty orders to his men.

"Get buckets and anything else you need to put out the fires. We need all the recruits we can—"

Some of the men screamed in horror. Kaspian turned to Brygida, his face pale, eyeing Matoha. Seated atop a goat demon, she must have looked like something out of their nightmares, but there was no time to placate them.

Most of them will be dead by dawn anyway. No need to concern yourself, Matoha commented in her head.

She groaned inwardly as she dismounted. Death is exactly what she aimed to prevent, Mokosza willing.

Kaspian jumped out of the saddle and rushed over to her, staring at Matoha warily. "Brygida, I tried to stop him, but the cult—they're going to burn the forest."

She grabbed his hands and squeezed. "I know, but someone needs to warn my mothers, and I cannot enter their witchlands."

"You want me?"

She nodded. Kaspian had a good heart. "Yes, I trust you."

He squeezed her hands back. "I will protect them with my life. But what about you?"

She glanced behind her at the pack of demons who had followed her here, skulking in the shadows. "I'm going to find the cultists."

CHAPTER 15

D eeper and deeper into the forest, Kaspian
took Demon along the worn deer path. He'd
walked to Brygida's cottage this same way
many times before, but the branches and brambles that
had once blocked his path, and the trees that had
closed in on all sides, were farther away than he
remembered. And the path was so much clearer than it
had once been, as if the overhanging branches and the
undergrowth had known he'd need swiftness to save
the lives of their caretakers.

He would warn Brygida's mothers, get them to
safety, and then he would deal with Henryk.

At the end of the path, the warm glow of the Mrok
cottage reflected on the restless waters of the lake.
Seeing it again, he felt the ghost of that skeletal hand

upon his face. And soon, that same water would become Henryk's grave.

He swung out of the saddle, and in a few strides, he was at the cottage door. He banged upon it, and the shuffle of footsteps approached. The door flew open, and an arrow pointed at his face.

"Don't make a move, or it will be your last." Ewa wore leather armor, and her auburn hair had been pulled back.

Kaspian put up his empty hands. "I didn't come to harm you. I came to get you out of the forest. The cult plans to burn the woods."

Liliana appeared at her partner's shoulder. "We know. We can feel the forest waking around us."

If they knew what was coming, why not run? It didn't matter what kept them here; all that mattered was getting them out now before it was too late. There was no more time. "If you don't run now, the cultists will come for you. They won't stop until you're dead."

"And we will meet them and defend our witchlands, as is our duty." Ewa lowered the bow at least, but her gaze continued to scan the forest behind him.

"I promised Brygida I would get you both to safety."

Liliana's gaze was fixed on the lake, and she took a step toward it. "A price must be paid."

Ewa grabbed her by the shoulder as she stepped out. "What are you saying? Is this your prophecy?"

Ravens cawed in the distance, and shouted voices echoed. They were getting closer.

"We can figure this out. We'll protect your forest, I promise, but for now, we need to protect *you*." Kaspian gestured toward the deer path that would lead them away.

Liliana grabbed onto Ewa's hands and met her gaze. "The cult is too strong, and even with the gift of water, my power is not enough. I need to go to the source."

The lake lapped against the bank, large ripples going outward and outward.

She couldn't mean the rusałki, could she? With them trapped inside this lake, other than luring Henryk here, there was no way the rusałki could do anything to help.

"No, it's too dangerous." Ewa grasped Liliana's wrists.

Liliana leaned forward, pressed a kiss to Ewa's lips, and then very gently, she pulled away before turning toward the lake.

"We don't have time. We need to go," Kaspian said.

But Liliana did not seem to hear him. Instead, she walked into the water. Each step hardly made a ripple as she went deeper and deeper.

"What is she doing?" Kaspian asked Ewa as Liliana reached waist-deep water.

Something white skimmed the surface of the water, circling her but not surfacing. He'd seen what was in those depths, and he would never go near it again if he had the choice. But he'd made Brygida a promise. He took a step forward, but Ewa pulled him back.

"She's going to the rusałki," Ewa said, her voice hoarse.

"What?" He spun.

Liliana was to her shoulders now. He couldn't just let her die!

"Stop!" He yanked his arm from Ewa's grasp, kicked off his boots, and waded in after Liliana.

Before he could get very far, Ewa grabbed him by the shoulders, pulling him back. "You cannot interfere. This is between Liliana and her ancestor, Iga Mrok."

Ewa's turbulent gaze fixed on Liliana as her head sank below the water. Her pale hair floated on the surface for a moment, before it too was consumed by the inky depths.

"Are you mad? She's going to drown down there."

Ewa's lips were drawn in a line as she stared at the water, her arms wrapped around her torso.

A shout came from the distance. He could almost make out their voices. The cult?

He looked back to the water. There was no sign of Liliana.

She would have to come up for air sometime. He held his own breath in anticipation. Seconds turned to minutes, and she didn't resurface.

No air.

She wasn't coming up for air.

Liliana—

Squeezing his eyes shut, he raked his hair back, doubling over. Perun's bright lightning, when Brygida needed him most, he couldn't even save her mothers.

Liliana wasn't coming back. Brygida's mother was gone. And he had allowed her to kill herself. Had stood by and watched it happen.

The thought struck him hard, but there wasn't time to process. Liliana had made her choice, but that didn't mean he had to leave Ewa to her fate.

He grasped her by the wrist. "They're coming. We have to go."

Ewa knocked his hand aside. "I'm not going anywhere, not until Liliana resurfaces."

"She's been down there much too long. She's not coming back. Please don't let Brygida lose both of her mothers. Please, Ewa."

She scowled at him. "You might doubt, but I know my love." She turned her gaze back to the water.

The water was still, as if even it were grieving.

Ewa was too stubborn to see reason, but if he couldn't drag her away, then he had only one other choice: to stop the cultists from setting the forest on fire, no matter what.

CHAPTER 16

H er heart thundering, Brygida pushed open the door to the Duma Inn. Her gaze snapped from each corner of the tavern to the next. Not a cultist in sight.

She blew out a breath through her nose, rubbing the crescent mark on her hand. With Mokosza's favor, she'd been able to track by blood, but with this? There had to be a way to find the cultists faster than searching every stretch of forest bordering Czarnobrzeg.

"By Her thread, Reaper," a familiar voice greeted. Bogdan.

He and his companion Gerard sat beside the roaring fireplace. Unlike the first time she had met them, there were no easy smiles on their faces. She made her way over to them.

"Have you come to Reap Agata's killer?" Gerard

asked with a fierce expression. "That cultist bastard should pay for what he did to Agata. She didn't deserve what was done to her."

They both shook their heads and grasped empty tankards. Firelight flickered off the pewter. When she had come searching for Roksana's killer, they had been instrumental in her discovering the real killer. And by their own admission, they'd spent more time in this tavern than anyone else.

"I'm looking for the cultists. Do you know where they might be gathered?"

"They used to be here all the time, before Agata rightly tossed them out," Bogdan said with a sad look back at the empty tavern. The entirety of the Duma Inn felt subdued and lacking in color. Even the flickering candlelight on the walls felt muted and lacking in warmth.

Knowing where the cultists had been before didn't help her now, however. She had to find them and stop them before they hurt more people.

"Do you know where they could have gone?" she asked.

The two men shared a look. "If we knew who killed Agata, we would have taken matters into our own hands, if you know what I mean," Gerard said coldly.

"But no one saw anything, or where those bastards slunk away to after they escaped the lord," Bogdan added.

Although she appreciated the sentiment, their desire for revenge wasn't enough. The cultists had to have allies somewhere in the village, someplace they were gathering. There was too much forest edge to investigate, and time was of the essence. She looked back to the door.

"I just can't believe those boys from the Malicki farm would turn out this way."

She turned back. "Malicki... You mean Roksana's family?"

Bogdan nodded. "Yeah, a couple of them kept spouting off nonsense about how Lord Rubin killed that poor girl."

"They were close with Julian, couldn't believe he'd do something so vile. But I always said that he was trouble. He had that look to him. Evil eye," said Gerard.

"And the Malicki family was fine with this behavior?" Brygida asked.

They both shifted uncomfortably in their seats. "Well, they've been through a lot, losing their girl and all."

"Albert is a good man, you hear me. But he hasn't been quite right since Roksana..."

That was it. They had to be using the Malicki farm as a staging area. It was something at least, when she had nothing to go on.

"By Her thread!" Brygida shouted and rushed for the door.

Outside, the sun had already started to set, and the sky was a burnt orange.

The Malicki farm was far away from the village square, past the manor even. Focusing on the thrum of the mark on her hand, she called Matoha, and in a few heart beats, she felt him respond.

An unearthly roar echoed through the dying light of day, and the villagers who were gathered in the square jumped out of Matoha's way. He knelt before her. *Let's go.*

She brushed his ebony ridge of fur and met his red eyes.

The villagers who were standing by grasped at their Mokosza stones and stared wide eyed as Brygida swung onto his back, coiled muscle and power.

Hold on tight, Matoha said before he took off flying, leaping higher than a horse. They raced together toward the Malicki farm and, she hoped, to where the cultists gathered.

෨෴෨

DEMON'S HOOVES TORE UP THE DIRT ALONGSIDE THE DARK shadowy forest, but Kaspian urged him faster. Time fled quickly, but he had a chance, a sliver of one, to stop this.

The sun had already set as he raced to the cross-roads where Stefan and the guards were waiting.

"Have you found them?" Kaspian asked as he pulled

back on Demon's reins. Demon bucked backward and then danced in place.

"They're gathering at the Malicki farm, and they've got guards everywhere. Getting through won't be easy."

"You don't have to—"

"Don't even finish that sentence." Stefan wagged a finger at him. "These are my people, too. I'm not going to turn my back on them."

Kaspian nodded. That was right. Witch or villager, they were all one community, and no one deserved to be persecuted.

The guards assembled, and with instructions to take prisoners wherever possible, they marched for the Malicki farm. How many times had he walked this path over his life, and he'd never thought he would be going there to make war.

The night-cloaked road gave them ample cover to prepare their attack. As they approached the gate, the Malicki farm's defenses came into view. Several armed cultists in black stood guard, among them farm hands he recognized, who'd worked for the Malicki family. In the distance, beyond the guards, numerous torches blinked, casting ambient light on the ground like fallen stars.

It was time.

With a gesture, Kaspian signaled to the guards to attack.

Creeping about in the shadows, they hid behind

trees and bushes as they made their way along fence lines, getting closer to the edge of the forest.

Crickets chirped, and the near-full moon cast an opalescent sheen over the dark landscape. As they got closer, someone snapped a branch.

A patrolling cultist stopped and stared into the gloom where he and his men were hidden. Kaspian held his breath; in the cultist's hand was a horn, one she could use to alert the others of their presence.

As the woman moved closer, Stefan—squatting in tall grass—crept faster and more quietly than he had ever seen.

Before the woman could shout, Stefan was upon her. He kept her locked in a hold until she passed out and crumpled to the ground.

Creeping low, Stefan returned to them once more.

"Where did you learn that?" Kaspian whispered.

Stefan shrugged. There was no more time to question.

As they got closer, he could clearly see Henryk. His hair like gold, he stood against the shadows of the forest, illuminated by the moonlight and the torches his followers held. The hum of voices carried on the night, but he couldn't make out the words.

With another gesture to his guards, Kaspian moved closer to the cultists gathering by the forest. Wind whistled through the trees, and the branches groaned.

Not for the first time, he felt as if the forest was

watching, but it was more hostile than before; perhaps it sensed Henryk's dark intentions. He had to stop Henryk before he unleashed its fury.

There was a single expanse between them, a fallow field, and there would be no more cover here. But a cloud rolled over the moon—Perun's favor—giving them the cover of darkness to make their final maneuver in secret.

As the guards got into place, all that was left was for Kaspian to give the signal. With a final nod, the guards sprang forward, catching the back of the crowd by surprise.

Kaspian shoved his way through the mayhem that ensued. To his right, Stefan moved with a speed and strength he'd never witnessed from him before. He took out two men, knocking their heads together as they slumped to the ground, and then threw his head back in a celebratory shout.

A woman rushed him, torch in hand. She swung it at him.

Kaspian jumped out of the way, narrowly avoiding a burn.

With a quick blow to her stomach, he subdued the cultist. She doubled over and fell to her knees.

At the back of the crowd, Henryk approached the forest, where kindling glistened with oil in the torchlight.

Kaspian rushed toward him. "Henryk, wait!"

Henryk held the torch aloft. "You shouldn't have crossed me, Kaspian. We could have been unstoppable together."

Kaspian held up his hands, moving slowly toward Henryk. "You don't need to do this. We can return to how things were."

There was a mad glint in Henryk's eyes as the flames flickered in his blue eyes. "Return?" He threw his head back. "Why would I ever want to return to you? You were always too soft, baby brother. Now I will do what must be done."

Henryk tossed the torch toward the trees.

As the torch spun through the air, Kaspian lurched forward, trying to catch it.

The torch fell into the kindling. The blaze burst upward, catching the trees. A glass shattered as a bottle of alcohol landed in the fire, spreading it further.

It was too late.

CHAPTER 17

Brygida leaned forward as Matoha flew over the fields and past farmhouses. His speed was both exhilarating and frightening as they sailed over fallen logs and cleared crumbling stone walls without breaking stride. The moon had risen, and it followed her progress.

The mark on her palm throbbed painfully as black mist continued to spill from it, leaving a trail of shadow in her wake.

A scream, neither human nor animal, filled her skull, rattling around inside her until her head pounded as if it would burst and her insides would liquefy. Her grip on Matoha loosened, and she fell from his back, hitting the ground hard.

She rolled onto a patch of grass, but jarred her shoulder and bashed her hip in the fall. The mark on her hand burned, and she clutched at it, writhing in agony as the screams of the forest filled her ears.

The demons too were hissing, growling, their voices angry and violent.

Kill. Kill. Kill.

Back arched, she clutched at the ground, scraping, searching for any sort of relief, anything to be free of the screams of the forest, the bloodlust of the demons. Hands digging into dirt, her spine curving, she let out a guttural scream that ripped her throat raw.

The cult had set fire to her witchlands.

The forest wasn't just awake; it was enraged. All its nightmares would be now made real, unleashed upon the world. So many demons, she could feel them, their voices crowding the inside of her head, filling her up to where she couldn't tell where they started and she began. She had to breathe, to grab some semblance of control, but the pain was too much, the burning in her mark moving up her arm, to her elbow and her shoulder.

The faces of the cultists flashed before her eyes, conveyed by the demons or the forest, she couldn't be certain. Their twisted, rage-filled expressions, the lick of flames, and the animalistic fear as the woods burned, burned, and burned... Hot tears blazed down her cheeks as she ripped tufts of grass out of the ground by the handful.

Kill. Kill. Kill.

The demons' voices kept chanting. Thick darkness dripped from her mark and onto the ground. The power was there, and she could use it, punish them, obliterate them, tear them to shreds until there was nothing left of them but bloody ribbons.

She rolled over, her face mashing into wet grass, and she inhaled. One after the other, she had to get control. Dragging muddy fingertips through the dirt, she rose up onto all fours. *Breathe in and then out.* The voices were fading, turning into a low hum, but the tightness of her chest did not cease. The urge—no, the compulsion to destroy, was like an itch under her skin, a twitching, wriggling insect burrowing and burrowing until it would drive her mad.

By sheer force of will, she sat back on her knees. The sky... It was illuminated by the amber glow of fire. Matoha stamped his foot, standing beside her.

He knelt down, allowing her to claw her way back onto his back. Her entire body was a trembling mess, and she could hardly grip even a tuft of his coarse fur.

The cultists...

To end this, she would have to kill them, no matter that it twisted her up, that it stood against everything she believed in. There was no other way, was there?

Black smoke poured from her mark; she couldn't contain it. It swirled around her like a deadly fog.

The forest is awake. What will you do? Matoha moved to face her, red slitted goat eyes trained upon her. He was nothing but a blur before the pain of the forest screams.

"I have to kill the cultists," she said through clenched teeth.

Alone? Matoha's red eyes bored into hers.

For months she had lived alone, worked alone, eaten alone. And every time she had gone to the forest to tame a new demon, he had asked her that same question. In her all-consuming desire to regain Mokosza's favor, she had thought the price of paying for her transgressions was hers alone to bear.

But was she ever truly alone? Nikodem and Urszula had brought her food and kept her company; Matoha had guided her; and even the memories of Mama and Mamusia had led her every step of the way. And even now, Kaspian was inside that forest, risking his life to save her mothers.

The cultists were many, and if she gave in to this craving for death and vengeance, there would be no turning back. She couldn't stop the cultists and not risk harming innocent lives in the process. Not alone. But like the lichyj, the demons, once tamed, would not harm, would not slaughter, and could help her fight the cultists without killing them.

"If I tame the demons, can everyone be saved without loss of life?"

Matoha blinked his red demon eyes at her. As usual,

he would give her no answers. This was her decision to make.

Clenching her jaw through the pain, she veered from the path, away from the cultists' fire and toward the Perun-struck oak, where she could feel the demons calling to her. They'd gathered like a river ready to overflow its banks.

She rode toward it, and as the voices of the demons grew stronger, the shrieks of the forest grew fainter. And the pain in her head was replaced with a throbbing in her hand. The darkness pouring from it continued to build and build.

They waited for her at the edge of the forest, an array of creatures both big and small from the massive leszy to the little panki.

Some rushed toward her as she rode toward them, claws and fangs ready to tear her apart. But as they crashed into the darkness of her mark, one by one they stopped, bowing down before her.

The darkness slid among them, wrapping around them like black bindings. Matoha stood still beneath her, and as Brygida held up her hands, the voices all stilled, their inhuman eyes trained upon her, gold, red, black and myriad shades. Her arms trembled as she looked upon them.

These demons from the stories Mamusia had told during her childhood, demons she had encountered and had been taught to fear, and others she'd tamed in

Anita's witchlands, and even more creatures of the wood, both friendly and fearsome... All of them bowed to her.

Matoha's expression was as close to a smile as a goat could have, bearing his pointed teeth.

We are yours to command. What will you have us do? he said into her mind.

Plumes of gray smoke choked the sky, obscuring the luminescent full moon. She felt as if she'd been wrung out like an old rag, but there was still more work to do.

Tonight she would see this finished. "Tonight we save Czarnobrzeg!"

CHAPTER 18

Henryk rushed toward Kaspian, sword raised for a crown strike. Kaspian leaped backward to dodge his attack, but the flames on either side penned him in. The heat licked at his side as he dodged another swing of Henryk's blade.

When they'd been boys, they'd often sparred together. Never had Kaspian won against Henryk. Not even once. A voice inside of him was screaming at him to run, to save his own life.

But he could run no more. He'd have to fight not just the man before him, but the memory, the mountain of a figure he'd once looked up to, who had bested him at everything. But he wasn't that little boy anymore. In the years Henryk had been away, Kaspian had learned, had trained, had prepared.

He drew his sword and slashed at Henryk, their blades clashing together.

As they met in the center, Henryk smirked at him. "I see you've been practicing, but you know you can never beat me," Henryk gloated.

Kaspian shoved him, putting Henryk on the back foot, pushing him toward the flames that grew hotter and higher with every moment. "I don't want to kill you. Tell your people to lay down their arms."

With a crooked smile, Henryk glanced past him. Kaspian turned, just as one of the inquisitors rushed him, a dagger aimed at his back.

He raised his sword, but it wouldn't be fast enough.

He did anyway.

A sword pierced her stomach. She stumbled, grasping the edge of the blade and looking up at Kaspian with shock before slumping.

"That was close." His face blood splattered, Stefan removed his blade from the corpse. There was a strange glint in his eye, perhaps a trick of the light. Had his front teeth elongated to points? Were those claws tipping his hands?

Kaspian blinked a few times, trying to clear his vision. "Thanks for the rescue."

Henryk was gone.

"That rat is running away, I bet." Stefan balled his hands into fists.

A woman screamed. Across the yard, half a dozen inquisitors dragged Teresa and Albert, Roksana's parents, from their home, with blades to their throats. Albert, a mountain of a man, would have easily over-powered them, but one of the inquisitors pressed the blade's edge to Teresa's neck to keep him compliant.

In a nearby field, Henryk ran, his black cape flaring behind him as he headed for the edge of the village and freedom. While his cultists did his dirty work, he would escape. Henryk had always been able to run faster, jump higher, and do everything better than he could. And they both knew it.

Kaspian couldn't let him get away, but he couldn't leave Roksana's parents to the mercy of the cultists either.

"You save Teresa and Albert. I'm going after Henryk," Kaspian said to Stefan.

"Consider it done. Go capture the rat," Stefan said with a snarling tone he'd never heard him use before. Stefan sprinted off toward Teresa, Albert and the cultists.

Picking up the dagger from the ground, Kaspian tucked it behind his back before sprinting after Henryk, sword in hand.

Henryk tried to jump over a fence, but the cape he wore caught on it, giving Kaspian a chance to catch up.

As the distance closed between them, Henryk

looked over his shoulder, finally tore his cape free, and picked up the pace. Through the unplowed fields, Kaspian stumbled and slowed as Henryk pulled farther ahead.

Out of the dense trees alongside, a bull-like demon barreled out in front of Henryk. It roared, rearing back, red eyes blazing.

Henryk veered to the left, and the demon's cloven hooves ate up the field behind him.

Crouched, Kaspian followed at a distance and among the trees. If Henryk could lose sight of him, just long enough, then if the demon didn't finish off Henryk, he would.

Ahead, a hapless cow screamed, taking off at a run toward the village. The demon paused, turning in its direction, and then charged.

Momentarily safe, Henryk doubled over, panting, and looked around.

In the tree cover, Kaspian sidled past and closed in on Henryk. Behind him, where he and Henryk had come from, more demons roared as they came from the forest.

They were everywhere, tearing apart both cultists and his allies alike.

In front of Henryk, demons emerged, too, prowling among the stalks of rye.

This was what Henryk had done; he had brought

destruction to the innocent with his prejudice. The fire had spread here as well, and they were stuck between the demons and the burning forest.

His back against the blaze, Henryk turned to face Kaspian.

"There's nowhere else to run. I will show you mercy if you'll just put down your sword," Kaspian said.

"Mercy?" Henryk scoffed, his gaze snapping from the flames, to Kaspian, and then to the demons sweeping over the battlefield. Henryk leveled his sword at Kaspian. "You'll join your precious witches in the world below."

Kaspian lunged, thrusting forward with his blade. Henryk side-stepped, but Kaspian grabbed Henryk by his torn cape and pulled down, yanking him off his feet. He kept his back away from Henryk, careful to keep the dagger tucked there out of Henryk's reach.

With his blade pressed to Henryk's throat, he could kill him now and this would all be over. In the thick of battle with their leader dead, the cultists would dissipate. No more innocent lives need be lost. With Liliana gone, there was nothing to wait for, nothing to keep Henryk alive for anymore.

He should do it. Henryk had committed such horrible crimes without remorse. A rapist. A murderer. A seditionist. This monster was his brother, his first playmate, his one-time hero. This revolting monster.

His hands shook.

"I know you don't want to kill me, Kaspian. Let's discuss this," Henryk pleaded, his blue eyes glimmering in the glow from the burning forest.

In the square, Henryk had used his emotional appeals to deceive people. He wouldn't fall for it. He knew better now.

Kaspian pressed the tip of his sword closer to Henryk's throat, and a drop of red welled there. "I can't believe I ever looked up to you."

"I'm still the same brother you knew, Kaspian. I went down this path because of my anger and fear. I know I shouldn't have hurt those people, but once the cult had me, I couldn't stop. They would have killed me," Henryk said, his eyes watering. "I can show you who the true leader is. I was nothing but a mouthpiece, you have to believe me. We can be a family again. You don't have to do this..." He held out his hand for Kaspian to take.

His hands did shake, but now was the time if he was to do it. It had to be now.

But... what if he really had been a mouthpiece? What if there was further sedition, further deadly plots to unravel?

Could he forgive himself if he killed Henryk, only to see a larger war unleashed on his people? If Henryk did have further names to give up...

No, he had done too much damage. To everyone. This was out of his hands alone.

With a sharp exhalation, Kaspian took a step back. The fire burned hot in the forest behind him, the smoke thickening to stinging eyes and a hoarse throat. "Your life isn't mine to take. Get up and walk toward the manor. All the allied lords together will decide what to do with you."

Henryk propped himself up from behind, heaving a relieved sigh. "Thank you, little brother. I promise, I will be useful to you. I'll tell you everything you wish to know."

A flaming oak cracked nearby, groaning as it toppled.

Henryk rolled, tossing ash up into his eyes.

It stung and blinded him, burning hot pain. He stumbled, rubbing at his eyes, trying to get it out. Henryk shoved him to the ground and kicked away his sword.

"You always were too weak, too soft to do what needed to be done." Henryk tsked as he pressed a boot to Kaspian's neck.

He gasped as Henryk pressed down harder, and clawed at the boot to no avail.

"You would have made a perfect puppet. If only that bitch hadn't gotten to you first."

As Henryk pressed him into the ground, something poked into his back. The dagger.

The dagger he'd picked up was still tucked behind him, if only he could reach it...

Henryk leaned in close, cutting off his air with the pressure on his neck. "You know what I'm going to do? I'm going to dominate that bitch. A girl like her needs to know her place, under a man."

Fire burned through his veins, like the flames silhouetting Henryk's face.

His hand fumbled for the dagger.

As Brygida raced atop Matoha's back toward the battle, the demons followed after her, flanking her like an oncoming storm. Chaos had torn up the Malicki farm. Ash covered everything, shrouding it in gray. There was no way to tell who was a cultist or a Rubin guard. The metallic scent of blood carried on the air, and the demons' restless hunger abraded against her consciousness.

Even if she could tell the cultists apart from her allies, she wouldn't allow the demons to indulge in their blood lust. Enough people had died; she would end this with as little cost of human life as possible.

There was a rumble and a shout from afar, and Brygida looked over her shoulder. A second wave of cultists came from down the road. They charged, unafraid of her demon army.

The demons paced, ready to rend them apart. But if

any of these people who'd been deceived by the cult's lies were hurt, it would be her fault.

"Defeat all," Brygida commanded, "but kill none."

The demons hissed and whispered their displeasure, but they were not the masters here. She was.

There was only one person here who would fall, and that was the Dog of Weles. The demons spread out around her, the enormous stag-like lejinie acting as a shield around her as she raced through the crowd.

Some cultists dropped their weapons and fled, but even more rushed forward, attacking the panki who sprinted out between the lejinie, a sleuth of small bear demons charging for knees and thighs with gleaming-sharp claws and needling teeth. They swarmed cultists together, toppling them and crippling them with bites and strikes.

The cultists still outnumbered them, surrounding them on all sides.

Let us kill them, the demons pleaded as the cultists shot arrows and slashed at them with swords. The lichyj cried out as a cultist thrust a blade through its heart.

Turning away, Brygida pushed forward. Henryk was close by; she could feel it on her skin. Killing him was all that mattered, and then this battle would be over.

Where is the leader? she asked the demons.

A *lelek* soared high above the war-torn fields, flapping its massive green-feathered wings. *Here he is, Master.*

She followed the harsh whisper in her mind to the edge of a field.

There he was, Kaspian pinned beneath him, his boot on Kaspian's throat. *No!*

Brygida rushed toward him, but as she neared, a group of inquisitors crept in, armed with bows and other weapons.

She had sworn she wouldn't kill women, no matter what heinous crimes they had done. Their fates weren't hers to decide.

"Out of my way!" she shouted, and her voice boomed with the harmony of a hundred demons.

"All witches must die." An inquisitor aimed her arrow at Brygida.

Before the inquisitor's arrow could fly, however, one embedded in her skull and she fell to the ground.

Mama stood at the edge of the forest, bow in hand.

"Go. I'll take care of them." Mama nodded toward where Henryk and Kaspian wrestled.

"I can't leave you alone!"

"I'm not." Mama nodded toward the distance, where a banner flew in front of a troop of warriors, Nikodem at the helm. Lord Granat's army had come with reinforcements. They were saved.

The army charged in, their blades meeting those of the cultists in a cacophony.

Brygida urged Matoha on, and he leaped over the

heads of the inquisitors, racing closer to where Henryk pinned Kaspian with his boot.

She leaped off Matoha's back, the black mist pouring from her hand, forming a thick ring around her. Henryk turned as she approached.

"Come a step closer and I'll kill him." Henryk pressed down harder upon Kaspian's windpipe. A thin rasp came from Kaspian's throat.

The dark mark throbbed as she gathered more of the shadows, shrouded herself in them like a cloak. *Flank him, those of you who can do so silently,* she ordered the demons.

Just another moment. She only needed to bide her time.

Behind her, the greater demons hissed and paced. Their presence would keep the cultists away.

Henryk's crazed eyes flickered toward the demons behind her, and then the furrows in the fields, the ears of rye swaying with her thralls' movements.

On the ground, Kaspian reached for something, but his fingers fumbled, grasping.

Henryk narrowed his eyes. "Do you think you can outmaneuver me? I have turned the entirety of Nizina to the cult. You and your blasphemous witchcraft cannot hope to defeat me."

"If you're not afraid, let Kaspian go, then," Brygida taunted.

He smirked. "I see the game you're playing—"

Kaspian stabbed a dagger into Henryk's thigh.

Henryk growled and jumped away while Kaspian scrambled to his feet. As Henryk lunged for Kaspian, Brygida sent out a tendril of her dark power, a snake of black mist sweeping to coil up around Henryk, wrapping him from the ground up. As the mist began to squeeze, Brygida felt a familiar tingle.

The darkness felt as the wrath once had.

It was not something to fear, but a gift, only it was a gift from Weles rather than Mokosza. Somewhere in the space between worlds, there was a gap, a crack where light and shadows commingled, and it was here that her power resided.

She was the Perun-struck oak.

She inhabited the boundary between worlds: she was a Mrok witch by blood, but she was the chosen of Weles and Mokosza both.

Raising her hand, she willed the darkness up to his face.

The glow of the burning forest dimmed.

The screams went silent.

A rush came from the forest, like the hum of the river.

The back of her neck prickled as she looked toward the trees.

A great black shadow rose up above the treetops, partially hidden behind a great cloud of gray smoke. Water rushed, roaring toward them.

Mamusia emerged from the smoldering, smoking forest, behind her a dark tide that rose up higher than the canopy, and in her hand the Scythe of the Mother.

But as the water began to descend, preparing to crash down upon them, out of the falling crest surfaced innumerable half-skeletal women, with their inky, seaweed-tangled hair, riding that wave with her.

The rusałki.

Bound up in dark tendrils, Henryk's eyes grew wide. "What in the Darkness's name is that?" Henryk pointed at the skeletal hands reaching out from the wave of water rolling toward them.

Kaspian smirked. "Your destruction."

Brygida leaped toward Kaspian, tackling him into her embrace, willing the demons to protect them. "Pray," she whispered to him, as his arms closed around her.

The demons behind her and those who'd tried to flank Henryk closed ranks around them, a living wall of demon flesh stemming the tide.

The rusałki rode in on black waves, sweeping up male targets as they desired while the water continued to flood the fields. An otherworldly song rose up among them, sounding the way a shiver felt, and men turned to them, mesmerized.

Their skeletal bodies swelled to beguiling maidenly beauty, their hair sleeked, and ghostly blossoms budded and bloomed along their paths, born of water and dying to it in cycles of rebirth.

It was beautiful and terrifying all at once. "Don't look," she breathed to Kaspian, but as she peered up from his hold, his gaze stayed only on her face.

"I couldn't stop if I tried." The ethereal black sea fell over the landscape, washing away the fire and crashing over those who fought. "Especially if this is when last I see."

Some turned and fled, others remained struggling against one another, and coursing through the waters were the rusałki. They grasped at the male cultists, pulling them down below the black waves, drowning them in shallow waters.

At the head was Mamusia, who glowed with a midnight-blue power. She glided atop a wave toward a darkness-bound Henryk, and as she neared, she held out her Scythe of the Mother, feathering the dark waters with its sharp point.

Black oozed from his nose as she met him eye to eye, and grasped his face in her hand, hooking the scythe behind his head.

Mamusia turned in her direction with serene eyes, waiting there, Henryk in her grasp.

Henryk was Mokosza's to take. For Agata. For Dorota. For the countless women who'd died to his beliefs.

Brygida nodded to her, and with a slow exhale,

called back the tendrils of black mist. As they descended, Mamusia lowered the scythe to the sound of his frenzied cries. Together with Henryk, she disappeared beneath the midnight waters, in a last flicker of moonlight her fair face gaunt, ghostly, gruesome.

CHAPTER 19

Awash in black waters, Kaspian was soaked but alive. His throat ached where Henryk's boot had nearly crushed his windpipe.

As the waters receded, Henryk's body lay on the ground like a broken toy. His sightless eyes stared up at the dark night sky. Henryk was dead.

Brygida stood over his body, panting for breath, and Kaspian stood up on swaying feet. Demons flanked her, the forest steamed, and beyond them, Lord Granat's army pushed back those cultists who continued to fight even though their leader was gone.

Brygida came over to him and took his hand in hers.

The receding water revealed the rusałki, crowned with grass and dark wet hair, whose skeletal hands gathered Henryk up.

Brygida bowed her head, and joining the rusałki,

she took Henryk's body and followed the tide of water back toward the forest.

"Is it really over?" His voice was not much more than a croak.

"Yes, he's gone," Brygida whispered. Demons trailed her to the forest. At the forest's edge, she paused, peering at her feet before looking ahead to the rusałki. The goat demon stopped beside her, tossing its enormous sharp-toothed head.

As one, the rusałki looked over their shoulders at her and nodded.

Brygida stepped over the threshold, and the demons with her dissipated like morning mist.

A new day, a fresh start.

"I can come home," she said softly, gasping her relief, and wiped at her face.

He canted his head. "Does that mean you're staying—"

"You're alive!" Stefan was covered in blood, but ran to them, splashing through muddy puddles. When he reached them, he threw his arms around their necks, bringing them both into a three-way embrace.

As they did, a downpour fell from the sky overhead.

"I don't know why I insist on protecting the two of you when you seem so damned determined to get me killed," Stefan said as rain streamed over his face, washing away the blood and dirt.

Brygida tilted her head back, letting the rainwater

run over her face and soak her hair. Kaspian pulled them both close as a laugh escaped his lips. They'd done it. After all they'd been through, all three of them had made it out alive.

Behind Stefan, Lord Granat's army surrounded the cultists. Henryk was dead. The battle was won. The village was safe.

Brygida popped her head up, her violet eyes gleaming alight. She ducked under Stefan's arm and ran toward Lord Granat's army.

There, Ewa and Liliana tended the wounds of the injured, of which there were many. Among them were Roksana's parents, who—other than a few scrapes—looked unharmed. Brygida tackled her mothers, who hugged her back, looking her over.

Under the shroud of night, Liliana had ridden a black wave with an army of rusałki, but in the light of the new dawn, she appeared the same as ever.

"I'm not sure I can make sense of what I saw in the night," he confessed to Stefan, who shrugged.

"Brygida called a horde of demons, her one mother turned into a rusałka, and her other mother shot people in the face with arrows. And an army came when most of the work was done to clean up," Stefan summarized.

Kaspian rolled his eyes. "What would I do without you?"

"Probably be dead, in case you're handing out accolades." Stefan dragged a bloodied arm across his forehead and sniffed. At least it didn't seem to be his blood.

All jesting aside, Stefan had acquitted himself capably, more so even than some of the guards. "Are you looking to become a man-at-arms?"

Another shrug. "Does it pay more?"

Together, they made their way to where Lord Granat had gathered all the cultists who had surrendered, but covered in mud and ash, they were difficult to tell apart.

Lord Granat, Nikodem, and Urszula were ordering soldiers and organizing the line of cultists who had been captured. Brygida joined him, and then Nikodem came over with her, his helmet under his arm.

If she was with Nikodem, he shouldn't push any boundaries. If it hadn't been for Granat's reinforcements, then the cultists might have turned the tide against them.

The grim reality was that he had survived, but many more hadn't been so lucky. The dead were strewn across the battlefield, rain washing away the blood and mingling it with the mud.

"All of the cultists have been captured. What do you believe we should do with them?" Nikodem, his golden hair soaked in blood and his leather jerkin slashed in multiple places, had clearly seen battle.

The inquisitors, who'd done the worst to innocent

people and the witches, should pay for what they'd done. But for the rest, he was less certain. They'd all fallen under Henryk's spell, deceived by his clever words, and had their beliefs twisted to meet his own ends. They didn't deserve to pay for Henryk's crimes, at least not lethally.

But this wasn't just his decision to make. It wasn't just he who'd been hunted and persecuted by the Cult of Weles.

"What do you say?" Kaspian asked Brygida.

Brygida looked across the sea of people in front of them, her violet eyes thoughtful. "I say we show them mercy. It is not our place to decide who lives and who dies. Let them redeem themselves and repay the evil they've done with good."

He nodded. Punishing these people who'd fallen under Henryk's spell would only breed more hatred, and punishing them too harshly would cause more divisions among the people of Nizina. Let the stain of the Cult of the Weles end with Henryk.

They had cut off the head off the serpent; no more needed to die. It was over.

With Brygida and Stefan behind him, he stepped up to face the assembled people.

"Your leader is dead," Kaspian announced, echoed by a sudden thunder that accompanied the proclamation, as if Perun himself was here to ensure justice would be done.

The inquisitors wailed, some collapsing into the mud, but the rest looked on with gaping mouths.

"My brother twisted your thoughts and actions, fueled by his own greed, hatred, and prejudice. For what you did by his command, I should see all of you executed for your crimes."

There was a general outcry, voices rising up, begging for mercy. Only the inquisitors in their high-collared black uniforms continued to cry, pleading for the Darkness to save them. The hearts of men and women were weak and easily swayed; Henryk had seen that and twisted it to his own ends. Seeing the fear on these people's faces, he knew they could be saved.

Kaspian held up his hand to silence them. The voices trailed off but for the wailing of the inquisitors. "But I believe hatred and vengeance breed only more of the same. And therefore I will give you this one chance. Put down your weapons, and repent your misdeeds. Dedicate your lives to the temples of Mokosza and Perun."

There was a pause, a few heart beats, as he waited for the cultists who surrounded them to decide what they would do.

As the rain poured down, one by one they removed the last remnants of the pins and trappings of the Cult of Weles. This was only the beginning of the hatred and fear that had been the perfect breeding ground for this cult. It could not be healed by one speech, but it was a start. And like the burning of a field affected by blight, he would do whatever was necessary to make sure that the Cult of Weles never returned.

The prisoners were taken away. The work had only just begun; there were bodies of the fallen to tend and the injured to be treated. There would be much to rebuild, but for now he was satisfied.

Liliana and Ewa approached, and Brygida threw her arms around them once more. Seeing her reunited with her mothers at last made his heart swell. As much as they'd lost, at least she was back where she belonged.

Stefan patted his shoulder before joining the restoration efforts, and he was prepared to join him when Liliana called out to him.

"Don't go." Liliana beckoned him closer.

Kaspian approached them cautiously. The three of them stood together, hands clasped, a family reunited once more.

"Thank you both for your help today. I am forever in your debt." Hate and misunderstanding of the witches had led them here, but going forward he would make sure they had a place among his people. The villagers and the witches would better understand each other.

"There's no need to thank us. Isn't that right, Ewa?" Liliana gave her a sly look.

Ewa cleared her throat. "Yes. If you had not come to warn us or fight to protect us..." She cleared her throat. "Anyway, I misjudged you, and I'm sorry."

His throat caught; he hadn't realized just how much he'd desired her approval. Perhaps it was too late for him and Brygida, since she had Nikodem, but maybe it would make relations between the village and the witches easier. "You don't need to thank me. We are all one community, after all." He rubbed the back of his neck.

"Just take the compliment," Ewa groused.

"Ewa—" Liliana scolded, hands on her hips.

And Ewa gave him a rare smile, perhaps the first one he'd ever seen from her. "You're a good man, and will be a great lord."

Brygida and Liliana beamed at him, as if this moment wasn't surreal enough to hear those words from Ewa. He felt as if he were moving through a waking dream.

"Thank you." He bowed his head to them, unsure of what else to do.

"And Brygida, the time has come. You can return home," Liliana said. "If it is your wish, you may rededicate yourself to Mokosza."

It was a bittersweet moment. Everything was returning to how it had been, everything in its place, she back in her world, and he in his.

"I will rededicate myself to Mokosza." Brygida held out her hand to him. "And I'd like Kaspian to witness it."

He did a double take, and Ewa frowned.

"Why not?" Liliana replied with a happy shrug, looking at him inquisitively.

He blinked a few times before nodding slowly. "Yes, it would be my honor."

෯෯෯

As Brygida crossed into her witchlands, she hesitated, if only for a moment. Turning up her palm, she looked down at the crescent-shaped mark. It remained. But as she got closer, the whispered voices of the wood filled her mind.

She pressed her hand against an oak, felt the pulse of the forest. The lifeblood of the sacred witchlands. And although it felt restless, it was the tossing and turning of a forest going back to sleep. Weles's mark remained, but her witchlands had accepted her, and now she was ready to rededicate herself to her goddess.

Mama and Mamusia went ahead, while Kaspian hung back with her.

"Everything all right?" he asked.

She smiled at him. It felt like just yesterday when the two of them had wandered these woods together, daydreaming and thinking nothing could ever divide them. Perhaps they hadn't been all that wrong, as here they were, undivided.

There was a smudge on Kaspian's cheek and a hollow to his cheeks, a darkness that lingered around him—the mantle of the heavy burden upon him as the lord of Rubin, and perhaps the truth that his brother was dead. But beneath all that was the painter she remembered that day in the forest, who'd first approached her with awe and wonder.

She could not imagine doing this without him by her side.

In the shadows tucked between two oaks, Matoha regarded her, his red eyes trained upon her. He bowed his head.

"One moment." Excusing herself, she jogged over to Matoha.

You've passed your challenge and earned a place among these sacred witchlands, Matoha spoke into her mind. Perhaps she was just imagining it, but there was a certain pride to his voice.

From the beginning, Matoha had been beside her, urging her to use her dark power, whispering about vengeance and blood. And each time she had resisted the temptation to kill without regard, without thought to the cost of human life. Had it been her challenge all along?

Matoha demons were known to punish witches who harmed the innocent, and while the Cult of Weles had been evil, not all of its followers had. Some had been coerced, some brainwashed, and others too feeble minded to fight back. Many had died for it, but the power of the truth had prevailed.

"But the mark is still here." Brygida looked to Matoha, holding up her hand.

And so it shall remain for the rest of your days. You are no longer just a servant of Mokosza but of one of her consorts —Weles—also. And as Mokosza goes from Perun to Weles and back again, so you shall live a split life in both light and shadow.

Brygida looked back at Kaspian, who stared at Matoha with wide eyes.

Matoha bowed his horned head once more before disappearing into the forest.

Up ahead, Mama and Mamusia waited. If they had seen Matoha, they'd given no indication of it.

"What was that demon saying to you?" Kaspian asked her.

"He's been a sort of guide, you could say, and he came to say goodbye." She wasn't quite sure what it meant to live in the light and shadow. But Mokosza did have two consorts, Perun—with whom She spent the spring and summer—and Weles, with whom She spent the fall and winter.

If she was to believe Matoha, her life would also be split between two worlds. But she wasn't sure in what way the gods would call her, not yet.

He nodded. "You must be glad to come home to your mothers. Will you stay here with them or leave with Nikodem?"

She frowned. "I'm not sure yet. I will see how

Mokosza guides me, but I would like to stay close to my mothers." She wasn't sure what Nikodem had to do with any of this, however.

"Well, if you choose to stay, Nikodem will be disappointed, I'm sure," Kaspian continued.

She wrinkled her nose. "I suppose, but the witchlands I was on were not mine. I am a Mrok witch." She had calmed Anita's witchlands as best she could, but that wood hadn't chosen her; someday, it would choose its own witch.

Kaspian cleared his throat. "Yes, but it is difficult to be away from those we love."

Did he mean her mothers? Well, at home, she wouldn't have to be away from them, except when she'd spend time with him, if he were receptive.

It was a strange topic of conversation. She thought now that the battle was over and they had a few moments together, they might talk as they once had, but he kept insisting on talking about Nikodem...

"I mean, it would be difficult to be away from Nikodem, since you're in love with him." He gestured wildly with his hand.

Brygida barked a laugh. "No. I am not in love with him!"

Kaspian's eyebrows furrowed for a moment. "You're not together?"

"No." She shook her head. "We are friends."

Kaspian blinked, again and again, and then he

laughed loudly. "I assumed when you arrived together, and you dressed in noble fashion, that the two of you were... Well, I guess it doesn't matter now." He looked at her sheepishly through lowered lashes.

He'd thought she and Nikodem were lovers? Her cheeks heated.

Certainly, Nikodem was a handsome enough man, but her heart hadn't spoken to him the way it had to Kaspian. Not that he would've needed the affections of a witch, with those of his lover and his wife already.

Kaspian straightened. "Oh! And I'm not betrothed to Nina."

She grinned broadly. "I know that."

"You do?"

She nodded. "Yes. I assumed you said that to protect her from Henryk, or in the hopes of doing so. Nina hadn't been at the manor, nor looked at you with any sort of affection, and of course, Lady Rubin already told me how lonely you've been."

His lips pressed together into a thin line as his eyebrows shot up to his hairline. He dropped his gaze. "I'm not sure whether to feel embarrassed or thankful."

Probably thankful. It wasn't always easy to discuss one's feelings, or even identify them, so his mother had simplified matters greatly. And besides, there was no reason to be embarrassed by loneliness. She'd often felt it growing up and still did. Should that have been embarrassing?

A pair of birds flitted onto a nearby branch, chirping happily as she Kaspian passed beneath them with Kaspian.

"You can feel both, if you wish." She took his hand and pulled him flush against her side. "Tell me what else you feel."

He cleared his throat and rubbed the back of his neck. "Relief. Joy—"

"Love?"

He grinned at her, and it was as if the sun were coming out from behind the clouds. "Yes. Love."

Good. If they both felt the same, then it would make enjoying their lives together so much easier.

As they made their way through the forest, arm in arm, the voices of the wood and the whispers of demons spoke to her, together creating their own unique harmony.

At last, they reached the center of the forest. Here, the air shimmered and glowed.

The Hallow was a sacred place where the veil between the worlds of the living and the gods was at its thinnest. She had first visited this place when she'd had her first blood. It was then that she had dedicated her life to Mokosza, and today she would do so again.

She gave Kaspian's hand a squeeze as Mamusia embraced Mama, clinging tightly to one another before slowly letting go. And then Mamusia held out her hand to Brygida, and they stepped beyond the barrier into the Hallow together.

In this place, the air was charged and the hairs on the back of her neck stood on end. Sunlight fell through the canopy, dappling the small pool of water fed from an underground spring.

Brygida knelt at the water's edge. Across from the pool was a flower, half its petals in shadow, the other half reaching for the sun.

Together, she and Mamusia dipped their hands into the cold crystal-clear water and brought it to their lips, drinking down its comfort. And when she looked up, a spider rappelled down from above.

Perhaps it was Mokosza Herself come to greet her, or just Her messenger; either way it was a good sign. She was home and back exactly where she belonged—on her witchlands.

"You've done well, Brygida. I knew you would." Mamusia put an arm around her shoulder as they watched the spider spin its web.

Brygida leaned on Mamusia's shoulder, inhaling her lavender scent. She felt as if she was home at last.

"I couldn't have done it without you." She sat up. "How did you rally the rusałki?"

Mamusia gave Brygida her typical effervescent smile. "I begged for their aid, and they gave it in exchange for my nights. Each night, I must return to the water and join our ancestors there. That was their price."

Her chest tightened. The long nights without Mamusia humming at her loom, without her and Mama's chatter amongst themselves, would be cold.

"I have made my peace with it. I would have given up much, much more for your sake." Mamusia stroked Brygida's head, and she leaned into Mamusia's touch.

If Mamusia hadn't been willing to give it, then more lives would have been lost. Brygida leaned her head against Mamusia's shoulder again. Perhaps that was the nature of life. In all darkness there was light, and even in the light there was dark. And as she walked this path forward, she would do so not alone, but with the love and support of her family and the man she loved.

She turned away from the Hallow as she and Mamusia rose. Outside, Kaspian waited, holding out a hand for her.

At long last, she had found her place, the space between the two worlds where they could exist.

She took his hand.

CHAPTER 20

Over the next couple days, Kaspian was too busy to think about much else aside from last rites for the dead and the aftermath of the battle. There were endless meetings between Lord Granat, Nikodem, Urszula, Brygida, Mama, and himself as they all tried to navigate the delicate balance of the new world they found themselves in.

Ewa, Liliana, and Brygida had worked tirelessly, preparing the bodies for last rites and seeing to the injured, who were being housed inside the manor. The kitchen bustled, trying to feed Lord Granat's army and the sick, and all hands were put to some sort of work. Much to his surprise, the village had turned out to help. They came in shifts: women of the village tending to the ill, men helping to carry and burn the bodies, children helping to catch geese and chickens to feed everyone.

After many hard days and nights, the dead had all been laid to rest and Lord Granat's army was leaving. Kaspian came downstairs into the courtyard, where Mama and Lord Granat spoke, their heads pressed together.

Unlike the first time he'd seen them together, seeing them this way now felt right. Mama didn't speak of it, but he knew she grieved for Tata and even for Henryk, or who he could have been. When she was with Lord Granat, there was a light in her eyes and a smile on her face; she deserved joy.

Kaspian approached them, and Mama moved away from Lord Granat slightly.

Lord Granat greeted him with a bowed head. "Lord Rubin. I thank you for your hospitality."

"It is I who should be thankful. Had you not come when you did, all of Rubin might have been overrun by cultists."

He put his hand on Kaspian's shoulder. "Think nothing of it. We are one Nizina after all."

"It's too bad you're leaving so soon. I know we would both like it if you stayed," Kaspian said with a mischievous smile and a glance between the two of them.

"You cannot feed my army for much longer, but if you will have me, I would partake of your hospitality again soon." Lord Granat offered his hand for Kaspian to shake.

He took it, giving a firm shake, while Mama looked on, smiling. Perhaps once there had been time to grieve for their losses, and things were set right throughout all the regions, there would be a chance for Mama and Lord Granat to find their own happiness at last.

Lord Granat called out to his men to leave with one last lingering look to Mama, and then he marched out with his forces. Kaspian and Mama watched them go, her arm linked behind his back.

"I hope you and he will be happy together. You deserve to follow what your heart wants," Kaspian remarked to Mama.

She canted her head and looked at him. "I should be the one saying that to you." She tutted. "Who's the mother and who's the son here?"

He chuckled.

She rubbed his back. "But in all seriousness, I never should have stopped you from being with the person you loved. If I'd known it would have meant seeing that passion in you die..." She shook her head.

He squeezed her shoulder and pulled her closer. "You just wanted what's best for me."

"But I didn't know what was best for you. For either of you." Her expression darkened.

"Let's go for a walk, hm?" Kaspian took her hand in his. It had been years since they'd walked together like this, and Mama beamed at him. When he'd been a child, they'd often walked here together. It was here in these green fields that he'd first felt the urge to paint, to capture the way the sun danced across rolling hills, to immortalize the feelings that a sunset gave him.

"When you and Henryk were children, I wanted to give you both the world," Mama said. "You both were terribly spoiled, I'm afraid."

He squeezed her hand. Henryk's death, although justified, still hurt; he couldn't get his head around it. He imagined it was like losing a diseased limb—understanding its infection, needing it to be severed, and yet wondering how life could have been had it been right. But imagining his brother as someone who hadn't hurt people meant imagining an entirely different person. "I know, Mama."

Her small hand was swallowed up by his. For so long he had seen her as infallible, all knowing. But even she had made mistakes.

"By the time I realized what Henryk had become, it was too late," she said, with a sad shake of her head. "I should have seen the evil that was growing in him. I thought he could be saved, but in the end I was too late. Then when rulership fell to you, I was so afraid that your soft nature would be your downfall. But Kaspian, I almost lost you, too." She grasped him by both shoulders. "I want your happiness above all else. That's what matters to me. Don't give up on painting just because you're lord of Rubin. And don't let politics dictate who you love."

They embraced before turning to look across the fields. In the distance, the fields that had been burned by the blight now bloomed with red poppies. A symbol of hope, of a fresh start. Even from the ashes of those destroyed crops, there was still something to look forward to.

And with Mama's blessing, he knew exactly what he wanted to make of his future. He and Mama walked back to the manor.

Zofia was in the yard talking with Stefan when he arrived. As she turned to greet him, she walked over with a beaming smile.

"Zofia, what brings you here?" Kaspian asked.

She glanced over at Stefan, and a blush covered her face before she cleared her throat. "I came looking for Brygida, actually. Our last heifer gave birth to twin calves. I thought she might want to see them."

Twins. Surely that and the poppies were signs from Perun of good fortune for their future. Rubin had been struck hard, but there was hope for rebirth and a new life to start over again.

"I'll let her know." Kaspian nodded and slid a look to Stefan.

"Let me know what?" Brygida approached them with a bright smile, wiping her hands on her apron she wore over her dress.

Her chestnut hair was braided, but a few tendrils had escaped to frame her face. Once he had seen her as some mysterious and unknowable creature, but as he unveiled each layer of who she was, he only fell more deeply in love with her.

"Zofia has twin calves. Would you like to go see?" Kaspian blurted. Stefan snorted, and Kaspian's face heated. He still never failed to act like a complete fool around her.

Brygida smiled. "That would be lovely."

"Before you go," Mama said. "I'd like to speak with you, if I might?"

Brygida nodded, and the two walked off together. Kaspian watched them go, straining to see their expressions.

Stefan elbowed him gently. "Nosy, aren't we?"

Maybe they were sharing secrets about a certain stable hand and a widow. "I'll just ask Stryjek when he returns. Gossip is his preserve, as you well know."

Stefan cleared his throat, and Zofia blushed. But he wasn't going to tease them further. He should have noticed it sooner—it wasn't Nina Stefan had been visiting the Baran farm for.

Across the yard, Mama and Brygida embraced. That was a good sign, wasn't it?

They both returned with smiles on their faces.

"She's all yours," Mama said.

They said goodbye to Mama and Stefan and

followed Zofia to her farm, where they gave a cursory glance to the small newborn calves. They seemed so small, but full of energy and a promise of the future.

Afterward, he and Brygida took a walk around the forest edge as they used to do, in what felt like a past life. So much had changed, and yet so much had stayed the same. He offered her his arm, and they strolled over the fields together, walking in amiable silence.

In some ways, it felt like the months apart had never happened; in other ways, it felt as if years had passed. But all that mattered was knowing he never wanted to be away from Brygida again. And it appeared that wish could now come true.

When last he'd visited her and her mothers at their cottage, they'd prepared an early dinner of black *czarnina*, duck blood soup. Everyone in Nizina knew what it meant, from the noblest of families to the most isolated frontiersmen. At the home of a young maiden, a suitor seeking her hand would be served golden czarnina, without the duck's blood, to mean his proposal was rejected.

Witches didn't marry.

But Liliana, with Ewa harrumphing behind her, had handed him a bowl. Of black czarnina.

His face had gone cold and he'd about dropped it, but it had been real. Brygida had asked him what was wrong and checked him for illness.

Yes, everyone in Nizina knew what it meant, from

the noblest of families to the most isolated frontiers-men... except, it seemed, Brygida.

But having her mothers' and Mama's blessing, he knew what he would ask her now.

As they walked, they approached the Perun-struck oak. The branches bloomed with fresh green leaves, droplets of rain on its bark sparkling like gems. The jars of offerings clustered together, and Kaspian pushed them aside to sit down among them. "Join me?"

Brygida sat down beside him and leaned her head on his shoulder as they watched the golden glow of daylight fade on the horizon. His heart felt so full in that moment it might burst, and it raced as he tried to form the right words.

He cleared his throat. "Brygida, you... make me the person I've always wanted to be, the person I am when I'm with you. In the first couple months I knew you, I realized I wanted to be with you. And in the past few months we've been apart, I've realized I never want to be without you." He swallowed over the dryness in his mouth. "I... Will you marry me?"

Brygida went completely still next to him, her mouth opening and closing. She lifted a hand to her cheek. "Kaspian, I... It's just that witches don't marry."

He blinked, his breath caught. "Right, of course, I..." *Am a complete fool with you per usual.*

She leaned forward and kissed him, parting his lips with a hesitant sweetness, and then pulling away just as quickly. A rosy blush bloomed across her face. "Witches don't *marry*," she said with a beaming grin, "but from this day forward until we return to the dust from whence we came, I promise to love you, cherish you, and support you."

Promised to one another...

His heart full, he cupped her cheeks, pulling her close for a deeper kiss as her hands tangled in his hair. Never before had a moment felt more right, never before had he felt more complete.

When they broke apart, he repeated those same words back to her. "Brygida, from this day forward, until we return to the dust from whence we came, I promise to love you, cherish you, and support you. You, and no other."

He took her hand in his, intertwining their fingers.

EPILOGUE

Six months later

Brygida squeezed her eyes shut too tightly, but she was too excited to care. She'd finally see it, after all this time, and silence the thousand different images she's envisioned with the real one.

"You promise not to peek?" Kaspian whispered against her ear.

Even if she wanted to, she couldn't see anything past his hands covering her eyes. After weeks of him sneaking off to paint in secret, she'd been dying to see it.

"I promise I won't look." She laughed, leaning back into him as he led her into the room. He guided her in, and the sunlight coming through the windows warmed her face. The scent of fresh paint and the musky scent of the hearth filled her nostrils.

"Ready?"

"I told you I was!" Brygida bounced on her toes. Mokosza's great loom, he was teasing her, the cruel man. "Come on, I want to see!"

With a chuckle, Kaspian uncovered her eyes.

Before her was a large canvas covered in crimson, gold, and peach. Familiar faces smiled up at her: Kaspian and herself at the center, flanked on one side by Mama and Mamusia, and on the other, Sabina, Łukasz, and Stefan—and a smiling Roksana.

In front of Brygida and Kaspian were two children she didn't recognize.

She approached, her fingers hovering over the grinning faces of the children. A girl with golden-blond hair and violet eyes, and a boy with auburn hair and blue eyes.

Wrinkling her nose, Brygida put her hand on her round belly. They had a baby on the way, but who could the other child be? "Who are these two?"

Kaspian rubbed the back of his neck and laughed. "Liliana might have told me about a vision she had of our little ones."

Wait... Not little *one*, but *ones*? Her mouth dropped open.

He rested his palm over hers. On his hand, a tattoo of the Perun-struck oak matched her own, the symbol of the promise they'd made to one another. They gazed at the portrait together. Not all of Mamusia's visions came true, but somehow she thought this one just might. Her belly certainly was big enough for two little ones, she felt. Or three. Or five.

"My Lord, Lady Brygida, the others are waiting for you," a servant said from the doorway.

"I suppose we should go," Kaspian said, nuzzling her neck. "I never did get to dance with you at the last Feast of the Mother." He squeezed her tight.

Those memories of the year past felt distant in some ways and in others all too close. They'd lost a lot, but they'd gained so much as well. And she couldn't wait to ask Mamusia a hundred questions about her latest vision. "It's nearly sundown, and I'd like to see Mamusia today before she returns to the lake."

He nodded. They exited the solarium and headed out into the yard, where the village awaited, as did the carriage that would carry them into the village square.

The harvest had been plentiful, and all was well. Seeing as it was their first Feast of the Mother together, the villagers had thought it fitting that they act as representatives of the fall. Brygida wore the bright red of the harvest queen, the embodiment of Mokosza, and Kaspian matched her in bright gold, the harvest king, Perun.

The villagers cheered as they arrived. And Mama and Mamusia as well? Brygida waved a hand at them hurriedly, eager to jump from her seat and rush to them. Dressed in the Mrok violet-dyed dresses, they greeted her and Kaspian at the square.

"Twins?" Brygida asked Mamusia, who embraced her.

"Beautiful twins," Mamusia whispered, before handing Brygida the spool of Mokosza's thread. Unlike years past when the Mrok witches had done their rituals in solitude, they all would participate together. She and Kaspian had vowed that they would knit Rubin together, closer, in every way they could.

The procession rode through the village, and the people followed after singing songs, with the gęśla's notes carried on the night air in a merry tune. At the bank of the Skawa River, Brygida made the offering to Mokosza with the villagers around her.

As the thread went down the river, rain droplets fell from the sky, a small blessing; Mokosza was here among them as they celebrated Her bounty.

Not so long ago, Brygida had been singing in the forest, asking when her "fall" would arrive as it had for the maidens marrying that year. At last, it had arrived... but it was unlike anything she had ever imagined it would be, and so much better.

Her life wasn't exactly like everyone's, but it was exactly right for her. She had her mothers and her witchlands and her faith, and she had Kaspian, Czarnobrzeg, and their promise to each other.

After the ceremony, they retired to the square, where she and Kaspian danced until her feet ached. Kaspian helped her to a chair, where she drank a glass of cider beside Bogdan and Gerard.

Stefan danced with Zofia, spinning her round and round until her face flushed, while Nina spun in circles, arms outstretched, free and without worries.

Sabina and Lord Granat danced all night as if there were no one in the world but the two of them. When the drinking and dancing finished, the time came for Brygida to depart as well.

"Thank you all for your hard work this season. May our village continue to prosper," Kaspian told the villagers in closing of the night, and everyone cheered.

As the villagers started to file away, Sabina came over to say goodnight, followed by a prancing mass of white fluff—Iskra bounding along happily. "You must take care of yourself, eat properly and don't over-exert yourself in your delicate condition." Sabina took Brygida's hand in hers and squeezed.

"I promise I will be fine." Besides, Mama had already barely allowed her to take a step without advice for her and the baby.

"And you'll return to the manor when it's time for the baby to be born, won't you? I want to be there when my grandchildren come into the world."

Brygida smiled. "You will be there. I know it."

Sabina pulled her into an embrace while Iskra

jumped up on them, wagging her huge tail. "The manor is going to be a little less bright without you."

Brygida hugged her back. "I will miss you, too," she said, then gave Iskra's head a pat before the dog flopped against her mistress's side.

With their goodbyes said, Kaspian held out his hand for her to take. "Can I walk you home?"

"Always." They walked together through the moonlit night, in its chilly air that ushered in the fall. She shivered a bit.

Kaspian put his arm around her, rubbing her to warmth. "You're certain the babies won't come early?"

She smiled. Perhaps the only person who worried more than Mama and Sabina was Kaspian. "I'm certain."

"I'll be there every day to see you and talk to the babies, just in case."

Brygida rested her head on his shoulder. After living together for months in the manor, she would miss the feeling of his loving embrace each night.

But this was the nature of being a dual witch. As Mokosza split her time between Perun and Weles, so she would split her time between life at the manor and on her witchlands. When the winter winds came and the night got longer, she needed to soothe the forest as Mamusia spent more time among the rusałki.

And when her daughter arrived, she too would need to learn the way of the Mrok witch.

Brygida rested her hand on her belly again. Twins. She could still hardly believe it.

They'd reached the edge of the forest at last, and Kaspian held her in his arms at the border between worlds.

"The good thing about being apart is that I get to anticipate seeing you again," Kaspian said, dipping in for a kiss.

"I give you one night before you're trying to sleep at the cottage with me," she teased.

"Can you blame me? Perhaps I should just build a cottage at the edge of the forest so I won't be too far from you."

She smirked and leaned into him. "A place where we can live with one foot in each world?"

He raised her chin, holding her gaze locked with his. "Any world with you is the one I want to live in."

Together, they bridged the boundary between worlds, their hands joined, Perun-struck oaks made one.

THE END

AUTHORS' NOTE

This moment feels surreal. A little over six months ago, we each had the opportunity to submit to an anthology. That would've been fun, but you know what's even more fun? Two friends putting together their ideas like chocolate and peanut butter, combining them into something even greater (and delicious).

We set out to write a short story together, but it quickly became apparent that Brygida and Kaspian's journey could not be contained in just a few pages. Soon, we were falling in love with our precious little cinnamon-roll characters and their world. Creatively, neither of us has ever felt more fulfilled as we have working on Witch of the Lake; we just seem to comple-ment one another in ways neither of us ever imagined. Over these last six months, we've been on as much of a journey as Brygida and Kaspian.

We've got more we're working on together, but we can't think of a better way to end 2019 than with the conclusion to our first co-authored trilogy.

Of course, we couldn't have completed this journey alone. We owe a huge debt of gratitude to our friend and fantastic storyteller Jessica "J.M." Butler, without whose detailed feedback and support this book would simply not be. Also, thanks go to Katherine Bennet, Alisha Klapheke, and Emily Gorman, whose critiques on this trilogy have been a great help. Our production team: Deborah Nemeth, whose edits put us on the right track; Anthony S. Holabird, whose proofreading cleaned up our immense mess (any leftover typos are *our* mistakes, and not his); and K.D. Ritchie from Story-wrappers, whose considerable talents provided us with such stunning covers—we couldn't have done this without you!

And you, our readers: you're the reason we do this. Without you, this series—and our careers—wouldn't exist. Thank you so much for supporting us and indulging our crazy (maybe even encouraging it *mus-tache twirl*). We'll miss these two, but on to more adventures together!

And maybe even one featuring a certain snarky stable hand now of the wolfy persuasion?!

Sincerely,

Miranda & Nicolette

PRONUNCIATION GUIDE

- Agata Duma: "ah-GAH-tah DOO-mah"
- Albert Malicki: "AHL-behrt Mah-LEETS-kee"
- Albin: AHL-been
- Anatol Bilski: ah-NAH-tohl BEEL-skee
- Andrzej: "ON-dzhey"
- Ania: ON-nyah
- bies: "BYESS"
- błędnica: "bwend-NEETS-ah"
- Bogdan: "BOHG-dahn"
- Brygida Mrok: "brih-GHEE-dah Mrohk"
- chorobnik: "hoh-ROBE-neek"
- Czarnobrzeg: "char-NOH-bzheg"
- Dariusz Baran: "DAHR-yoosh BAH-rahn"
- Demon: "DEH-mon"
- Dażbóg: "DAHZH-boog"

- Dorota Duma: "doh-ROH-tah DOO-mah"
- drak: "DRAHK"
- Dziewanna: "djeh-VAHN-nah"
- Ewa Mrok: "EH-vah Mrohk"
- Gerard: "GHEH-rahrd"
- gęśla: "GHEWSCH-lah"
- Granat: "GRAH-not"
- Halina: "hah-LEE-nah"
- Henryk Wolski: "HEN-rihk VOHL-skee"
- Iga Mrok: "EE-gah Mrohk"
- Iskra: "EES-krah"
- Jadwiga: Yod-VEE-gah
- Julian Zając: "YOOL-yan ZAH-yohntz"
- Kaspian Wolski: "KAHS-pyahn VOHL-skee"
- Kolęda: "kohl-EN-dah"
- lasowik: "lah-SOH-veek"; [pl. lasowiki: "lah-soh-VEE- kee"]
- lejiń: "LEH-yeen"; [pl. lejinie: "leh-YEE-nyeh"]
- Lelek: LEH-lek
- leśna nimfa: "LESH-nah NEEM-fah"
- leszy: "LEH-shih" [pl. lesze: "LEH-sheh"]
- Lichyj: LEE-hiy
- Liliana Mrok: "leel-YAH-nah Mrohk"
- Łukasz Wolski: "WOO-kash VOHL-skee"
- Maciek: MAH-chek
- maleńka: "mah-LEN-kah"
- mamon: "mah-MOHN"

- Mamusia: "mah-MOO-shah"
- Marzanna: Mah-ZHAHN-nah
- Matoha: Mah-TOH-ha
- Mokosza: "Moh-KOH-shah"
- Mroczne: "MROCH-neh"
- Nikodem: "nee-KOH-dem"
- Nina Baran: "NEE-nah BAH-rahn"
- Nizina: "nee-ZEE-nah"
- Oskar Grobowski: "OHS-kahr groh-BOHF-skee"
- Owsiany koń: OHF-shonih KOHÑ
- Panek: PAH-nek
- Panki: PAHN-kee
- Perun: "PEH-roon"
- polewik: "poh-LEH-veek" [pl. polewiki: "Poh-leh-VEE-kee"]
- Rafał: "RAH-fahw"
- Roksana Malicka: "rok-SAH-nah mah-LEETS-kah"
- Rubin: "ROO-been"
- rusałka: "roo-SOW-kah" [pl. rusałki: "roo-SOW-kee"]
- Sabina Wolska: "sah-BEE-nah VOHL-skah"
- Skawa: "SKAH-vah"
- Stefan Bania: "STEH-fahn BAH-nyah"
- Stryjek: "STRIH-yek"
- Swaróg: "SFAH-roog"
- Szmaragd: SHMA-rogd

- Tarnowice: "rar-noh-VEE-tzeh"
- Tata: "TAH-tah"
- Teresa Malicka: "teh-REH-sah mah-LEETS-kah"
- Urszula: "ur-SHOO-lah"
- Wacek: VAH-tzek
- Weles: "VEL-es"
- Wilk: "VEELK"
- wilkołak: "veel-KOH-wok"
- Zofia Baran: "ZOHF-yah BAH-rahn"

BIBLIOGRAPHY

We couldn't have written this book without the wonderful resources, both in Polish and in English, on various historical and mythological aspects that helped us immensely.

Bobrowski, Jakub, Mateusz Wrona, and Błażej Ostoja-Lniski. *Czarty, Biesy, Zjawy: Opowieści z Pańskiego Stołu.* N.p.: Bosz, 2019. Print.

Bobrowski, Jakub, Mateusz Wrona, and Magdalena Boffito. *Mitologia Słowiańska.* N.p.: Wydawnictwo Bosz Szymanik i Wspólnicy, 2018. Print.

Cunningham, Scott. *Cunningham's Encyclopedia of Magical Herbs.* St. Paul, MN: Llewellyn Publications, 2016. Print.

Debuigne, Gérard, François Couplan, Pierre Vignes, Délia Vignes, and Katarzyna Cedro. *Wielki Zielnik Roślin Leczniczych*. Kielce: Wydawnictwo Jedność, 2019. Print.

Dębek, Bogusław Andrzej. *Początki Ludów: Europejczycy, Słowianie*. N.p.: Bellona, 2019. Print.

Gieysztor, Aleksander, Karol Modzelewski, Leszek Paweł Słupecki, and Aneta Pieniądz. *Mitologia Słowian*. N.p.: Wydawnictwa Uniwersytetu Warszawskiego, 2018. Print.

Kajkowski, Kamil. *Mity, Kult i Rytuał: O Duchowości Nadbałtyckich Słowian*. N.p.: Triglav, 2017. Print.

Knab, Sophie Hodorowicz. *Polish Customs, Traditions and Folklore*. New York: Hippocrene, 2017. Print.

Lehner, Ernst. *Folklore and Symbolism of Flowers, Plants and Trees*. Martino Fine, 2012. Print.

Moszyński, Kazimierz, and Jadwiga Klimaszewska. *Kultura Ludowa Słowian*. N.p.: Grafika Usługi Wydawnicze Iwona Knechta, 2010. Print.

Moszyński, Kazimierz, and Jadwiga Klimaszewska. *Kultura Ludowa Słowian*. N.p.: Grafika Usługi Wydawnicze Iwona Knechta, 2010. Print.

Moszyński, Kazimierz, Jadwiga Klimaszewska, and Maria Bytnar-Suboczowa. *Kultura Ludowa Słowian*. N.p.: Grafika Usługi Wydawnicze Iwona Knechta, 2010. Print.

Pankalla, Andrzej, and Konrad Kazimierz Kośnik. *Indygeniczna Psychologia Słowian: Wprowadzenie Do Realnej Nauki o Duszy*. N.p.: TAiWPN UNIVERSITAS, 2018. Print.

Pobiegły, Elżbieta, and Ewa Rossal. *Stroje Krakowskie: Historie i Mity: Praca Zbiorowa*. Krakow: Muzeum Etnograficzne Im. Seweryna Udzieli, 2017. Print.

Strzelczyk, Jerzy. *Bohaterowie Słowian Połabskich*. N.p.: Wydawnictwo Poznańskie, 2017. Print.

Szczepanik, Paweł. *Słowiańskie Zaświaty: Wierzenia, Wizje i Mity*. Szczecin: Triglav, 2018. Print.

Szrejter, Artur. *Pod Pogańskim Sztandarem: Dzieje Tysiąca Wojen Słowian Połabskich Od VII Do XII Wieku*. Warszawa: Instytut Wydawniczy Erica, 2016. Print.

Vargas, Witold, and Paweł Zych. *Magiczne Zawody: Kowal, Czarodziej, Alchemik*. N.p.: Bosz, 2018. Print.

Zielina, Jakub. *Wierzenia Prasłowian*. Kraków: Wydawnictwo Petrus, 2014. Print.

Zych, Paweł, and Witold Vargas. *Bestiariusz Słowiański.* N.p.: Bosz, 2018. Print.

ABOUT MIRANDA HONFLEUR

Miranda Honfleur is a born-and-raised Chicagoan living in Indianapolis. She grew up on fantasy and science fiction novels, spending nearly as much time in Valdemar, Pern, Tortall, Narnia, and Middle Earth as in reality.

In another life, her J.D. and M.B.A. were meant to serve a career in law, but now she gets to live her dream job: writing speculative fiction starring fierce heroines and daring heroes who make difficult choices along their adventures and intrigues, all with a generous (over)dose of romance.

When she's not snarking, writing, or reading her Kindle, she hangs out and watches Netflix with her English-teacher husband and plays board games with her friends.

Reach her at:
www.mirandahonfleur.com
miri@mirandahonfleur.com
https://www.patreon.com/honfleur

facebook.com/mirandahonfleur

twitter.com/MirandaHonfleur

amazon.com/author/mirandahonfleur

bookbub.com/authors/miranda-honfleur

goodreads.com/mirandahonfleur

instagram.com/mirandahonfleur

ABOUT NICOLETTE ANDREWS

Nicolette Andrews is a native San Diegan with a passion for the world of make-believe. From a young age, Nicolette was telling stories, whether it was writing plays for her friends to act out or making a series of children's books that her mother still likes drag out to embarrass her in front of company.

She still lives in her imagination, but in reality she resides in San Diego with her husband, children and a couple cats. She loves reading, attempting arts and crafts, and cooking.

You can visit her at her website:
www.fantasyauthornicoletteandrews.com
or at these places:

CPSIA information can be obtained
at www.ICGtesting.com
Printed in the USA
LVHW030855271220
675096LV00006B/841

9 781949 932225